BOTTLE ALLEY

BRENDA SPALDING

BOTTLE ALLEY

This books is dedicated to

Margaret Dennison Laroche

My friend for over sixty years still lives in "The Lake"

and has been a great help to me as I tried to remember the

names and places from the old days.

May God hold you in the palm of His hand.

Acknowledgements

I wish to thank my editors, Nancy Buscher for her help in developing the characters in the story and Clarissa Thomasson for her careful proof editing.

I also wish to thank members of ABCBooks4Children&Adults, Inc., my fellow members of the National League of American Pen Women for their interest and encouragement while I worked on the book and my friends at Art Center Sarasota who support my writing career and help me to spread my wings.

Several more friends and relatives supplied me with information in the writing of this novel.

You are all appreciated.

Forward

Newton, Massachusetts, in 1938 was a mix of Irish, Italian, French and Jewish. They were first and second generation immigrants looking for a better way of life in America.

The "Lake area" is in Nonantum, one of thirteen villages that make up the city of Newton. Researching my home area was a unique experience. I learned a lot about its historical beginnings and more about the people and places I knew as a child.

The story I have told is fictional. The basis of the story is one theory about the "Lake Language" and how it became incorporated into the everyday usage by the locals in the area.

I have used stories my father told me about his growing up in the "Lake." The old stories have been woven into the novel. The name "Bottle Alley" was the nickname for Adams Street.

In my father's day, children did gather coal from along the railway line. In my research I did find a peat bog on Hawthorn Street, and I remember skating on Silver Lake as a child. I grew up in a house on Chandler Street and have used the house as the home of the Flannigan Family. Fried's store was where we bought most of the clothes we needed until shopping malls arrived. Mazolla's bakery had the best fresh bread; the smell of the bread baking filled the neighborhood.

I went to the gypsy carnival at Our Lady's with my father. He won a bank in the shape of Peter Rabbit, made of plaster, which I kept for many years. "Our Lady Help of Christians" was my school from kindergarten to graduation from high school.

The hurricane is also true. It was called the "Long Island Express." It devastated Long Island, New York, and seven hundred lives were lost. It traveled at sixty miles an hour and was preceded by a week of heavy rain, wind and flooding. It crossed Western Massachusetts on its way to upstate New York and Canada.

I have created characters and families to bring the story of the "Lake" and its language to life. All names and characterizations are from my imagination and do not reflect on any real person alive or dead.

Lake Talk

Lake Talk is a cant spoken particularly among older Italian-American residents. The origins of Lake Talk are unclear, but it bears similarities to Angloromani or Italian Romany slang. One strong idea is that the language is a carryover from the traveling carnivals that roamed the country in the 1930's and 40's. The young locals worked the carnivals for extra money and used the strange language as a code of solidarity among them.

The language is still in use today and is being passed down to the younger children.

- *mush* (pronounced to rhyme with *push*) "guy" or "man" can be positive or negative depending on context
- *wicked pissa, mush!* "extremely awesome, man"
- *chor'd* "stolen," possibly related to the Romany word *choro* "thief"
- *chuccuo* (chu-co, also pronounced as "chew-ch") "donkey," "horse's ass"
- *cuyamoi* "shut up" or "go to hell"
- *divia* (div-ya) "crazy," "jerk, screw-up, or harmless screwball," can be used as a noun or an adjective: "The mush is a real divya," or "This mush is divya"
- *inga* "unattractive" or "bad-tempered person" or "junk" or "crap"
- *jival* "girl," female version of mush
- *mush has a cormunga in his cover* "guy is hiding a gun"
- *over-chay* or *overchay* (ova-chay) "it's a lie" or "he's an actor." Directly translates as "overkill." Better defined as exaggeration or equivocation
- *pukka to the mush* "tell the guy"
- *quisterjival* (quest-ah jival) "pretty girl"

- *quister* (also pronounced as "quish-ta") awesome, good, beautiful
- *quister mush* (quest-ah mush) "good, standup guy"
- *geech* "go away"
- *jawl* "steal" or "look at"
- *dikkikidotti* "unreal or unbelievable"

The mark of a true, old-school Lake resident is talent for the so-called Lake language — a collection of words and phrases believed to have roots in Romany, a language spoken by Gypsy immigrants from Europe, and brought back to the Lake early this century by local youths who worked for a time with traveling carnivals.

The Romany words mixed with Italian, English, and other street slang of the 1930s and '40s to produce a lively mix that is one of the strongest links to the Lake's proud and rough-and-tumble past.

Thanks go to the Wikipedia site on Nonantum, Massachusetts.

The Boston Globe article is: "They still speak the language of the Lake" Sept 13, 2009. The complete article is available on line.

CHAPTER ONE

"Hey, Mush!" Tony Pellegrino calls to Michael on the other side of the street. Lifelong friends, they've known one another since kindergarten, and now both young men work in the Aetna mill across the Charles River on Pleasant Street.

Newton, Massachusetts, in 1938 is a melting pot of Irish, Italian, Jewish, and French immigrants. Each holds fast to his culture. A French bakery next to an Italian deli and flanked by a Jewish tailor shop is not unusual. It is a friendly town where kids play together sharing their languages as well as their sandwiches.

Michael watches Tony dash across Watertown Street—dodging cars, and ignoring the honking and shouts of angry drivers. He shuffles the bag he's carrying to his other arm. Canned goods get heavy. "What, no work today? It's only Friday,"Michael says.

"Naw, I took the day off." Tony pulls out a Lucky Strike and lights it—exhaling slowly so the smoke makes almost perfect circles. He grins, and waits for a comment. When Michael doesn't respond, Tony continues, "I'm working at the carnival down at Our Lady's. Ya' comin'?"

"Can't, I'm working the night shift at the mill tonight. Probably because *you* took the day off," Michael answers, giving him a friendly punch. "Ma doesn't like us going to the carnivals anyways; says it's just a way to part a fool from his money."

"But it's at Our Lady's. Surely she can't find fault with that? Come on. You deserve some fun."

"I can't afford to pass up the work, Tony. Things are really tight at home."

"Then let's stop in Murphy's for a beer?"

"Ma needs me." Michael pauses as if considering. "No."After another pause, he grins, "She'll probably want me digging a new garden plot or cleaning out the chicken coop." Both snigger in agreement.

Tony crushes his cigarette out on the pavement. "Ok, you be the *momma's boy,* and I'll see ya' later. Oh, and tell Ellen I said hi, would ya'?"

"If you're so sweet on my sister, why don't you do something about it?"

"Come on, Ellen's different, ya' know. . . I don't wanna say the wrong thing. Hey, maybe she'd come with ya' tomorrow night?" Tony is charming. When he gets nervous, he drops his head, causing his dark hair to fall over his eyes. He's quick to brush it away.

"Ok, how about tomorrow night?" Tony persists.

"I can't. You know how Ma is."

Tony cocks an eyebrow and flashes his familiar cheeky grin.

"Aw, I'll try... Maybe I can think of a way, but don't count on it."

Tony's grin widens.

"And don't go getting involved with any of those carnival girls, hear me?" He pokes his friend; maybe a little harder than he intended. "They are bad news. I'm not kidding."

"Oh, geech, I can take care of myself. Don't worry."

"Yeah? Somebody'd better."

They have grown up together, been best pals since kindergarten, and in high school even chased the same girls, but trouble always seems to be around the corner waiting for Tony. His charm is only one of his gifts, and he has learned to use them all to his advantage.

"I won't promise anything, but I'll try."

"Good enough."

Tony and Michael go their separate ways. At the corner, Michael pauses before crossing Bridge Street. When he turns, he sees Tony go into Murphy's Tavern. He shakes his head. "Use some sense, Buddy," he says under his breath, ". . . and don't stay in there all afternoon."

He shifts the weight of the grocery bag again and crosses the street. It's half past twelve as a man staggers past him. The man catches himself and pauses blinking in the sunlight.

"Afternoon, Mr. Collins," Michael says in passing. *Stayed too long in Sullivan's again,* Michael thinks to himself.

"Oh, yeah. Nice day." Collins straightens his jacket and tries to keep things in focus. "Uh, say 'ello to yur folks, Son."

"I'll do that, Sir."

He reaches the corner of Adams Street and shifts the weight of the bag again. 'The Lake area' of Newton is small, and most people know one another. St. Mary's is the biggest football rival of Our Lady's, but they are friendly rivals, of course. Father Sheridan wouldn't have it any other way. "Now, boys," he'd say, "you can beat the stuffin' out of them on Friday nights. But if I hear in confession you've hurt them any other time, your absolution will be tripled." And everyone knew he meant it.

15

"Yoo-hoo, Michael Flannigan!" calls a female voice. He looks up to see Sally Watson coming toward him. He waits for her to catch up. "I thought that was you. I called before, but I guess you didn't hear me."

"Sorry."

They stand on the sidewalk in front of Pasquale's barbershop. Sally is a sweet girl, a few years younger than him.

"Are you going to the carnival at Our Lady's?" Sally asks hopefully.

"I don't often see you without your friend Gladys," Michael says—changing the subject.

"We're not friends anymore. She's gone high hat since she started going out with that Harvard boy. She's turning into a gold digger."

"I'm sorry. I know you were friends a long time."

"She's a twit! Well, it was good running into you. I hope I'll see you at the carnival."

"Maybe."

"I'd better run, or I'll be late."

Watching her dash off, Michael turns to watch the red, white and blue barber pole spin around and around to a steady click, click, click before he moves on.

Michael turns right onto Adams Street. As he walks, he hears tinny music coming from the open door to Sullivan's Tavern. The owner, Eddie, is wiping down the bar.

Looking up, Eddie calls, "Top o' the day to ya', Michael."

"I heard the music."

"You like it? It's new. It's a Victrola. Ya wind it up, and it plays music. Pretty good, huh?"

"It sure is, Mr. O'Dowd."

"Still got a few Irish Boxty, if you're hungry."

"No thanks. Ma is expecting me home. Maybe another time."

"How is your ma?" Eddie asks as he takes several items from a plate and wraps them in a clean bar towel. He comes around the bar and walks to the door. "No sense in wasting them. Take a few home to your Ma, Boy-o. They're fierce good. The missus made them this morning." He puts them in the bag Michael is carrying.

"Thank you, Mr. O'Dowd."

Sullivan's is where many of the parishioners from Our Lady stop for a drink and fish and chips on Fridays. Saturday night is a great night to enjoy some of the locals playing Irish music. To Michael it seems like every other building is a tavern or a brewery on Adams Street.

Small wonder the locals call this area "Bottle Alley," Michael thinks.

CHAPTER TWO

March 21, 1937, is a gray and chilly day as Donal Flannigan trudges toward Aetna Mill across the Charles River on Pleasant Street. The walk is familiar. It's one he's taken year after year. But today is different; he can feel it in his bones. He pulls the collar of his coat up around his ears to cut some of the wind. The din of machinery reaches him long before he gets to the gate. Inside the yard men cluster and quickly push through the large heavy doors that lead to the work area.

"Colder'n a well-diggers arse out there, Dave," he says to the shift supervisor as he clocks in and heads to the cloakroom. He removes his coat and hat and hangs them on the bar of hooks attached to the wall. Below are cubbyholes, and he drops his lunch bag in one.

"Donal!"

He turns to see Joseph waving a newspaper. "Wat'cha got there?" he shouts over the racket.

"There's a horse-shoe tournament next week over in Waltham. Can you make it?"

"I'll let'ch know," he calls back. "If ya' can't do any better than last time, I should stay home!" Joseph makes an obscene gesture, but he's grinning. Several men nearby guffaw; Donal waves to them as he moves to his station.

The mills provide jobs and help support the growing communities that spread up and down the river. People swim and fish in the water that is gradually being polluted by the factories along its banks. Workers are glad to have the jobs. The Depression has gone on too long. Everyone knows men who have been out of work for years, and even some who kissed it off. A working man knows the risks, though. Even so, people are sometimes maimed or even killed.

"Donal, we're runnin' behind. Can ya speed it up? That guard's what's slowin' things down. Just take the damn thing off," Dave shouts over the clang and clamor of the machines.

"Sure, Boss," Donal calls back. He pulls a pair of pliers off his work cart and loosens the bolts on the productive shield that separates the blades and rollers from the operator. No one thinks anything of it. Without the guard, the work speeds up by half. Time is money, and they are used to taking shortcuts.

Machines cut, slice, roll, and smash steadily all morning. The racket is deafening, but a guy gets used to it. After a while he doesn't notice the ringing in his ears at the end of a shift. Donal never gets headaches anymore. A guy gets used to it.

Just then Donal hears someone whistle and turns in time to see Rocky Snowden signal him.

"Can't hear ya," he calls back. Rocky mouths something, but it is lost in the cacophony of the labor.

"I can't hear ya! What?"

He looks up again for only a second before his attention is immediately drawn back to his machine. But it is too late. His left sleeve catches, and the material is pulled steadily into the rollers. Donal tries to wrench his sleeve clear—to no avail. He wants the material to tear so he can free his arm. The rhythm of the machine is constant; the pull is steady. To Donal it is like watching in slow motion as the rollers chew on. The sleeve disappears between the rollers—and with it his hand and then his wrist. There's no pain.

20

All he feels is the terror of what is happening. His arm is pulled into the grip of the menacing machine. Donal pulls frantically—twisting, and jerking. He might have cried out or said something like "oh, shit," but he isn't sure.

He pulls frantically and watches as the arm gradually vanishes between the rollers. Then he does scream, not from pain, but from sheer terror. Suddenly there are people all around. People are shouting, but he can't make out the words. Hands are on him, grabbing and pulling, trying to help, but the thing continues to eat his arm... past the elbow... up and up. Then everything stops. Silence fills the space as someone turns off the machine. The pandemonium fades away as Donal watches the rollers still clinging to his arm. Now he sees blood spreading from under the rollers. He feels an icy cold chill take over his body. The clamor fades, but all he hears is the ringing in his head. The voices fade completely as everything goes black.

". . . was nearly torn off at the shoulder. They got him out before that happened. Muscles are wrenched, and the nerve damage could be beyond repair. Only time will tell if he will ever get full use of the arm again. With a crush injury like this, we just never know." The doctor adjusts his glasses as he reads from the chart. "His back was wrenched severely when they tried to release him from the machine. He should consider himself lucky he's even alive. I'm sorry, Mrs. Flannigan. We did all we could."

Moira stands motionless as she tries to absorb all that's being said.

"Again, I'm sorry. He'll stay here for a few weeks so we can watch him. There will be therapy, of course, to help him walk. I can't give you any false hope. It's possible he may never walk again. He'll have to spend some time in the Sharon Sanitarium, where they have the staff to help him through this. He'll need to be closely watched for several months, but in time you will be able to take him home. You have help there, don't you? ...children who can assist with his care?"

Moira nods.

"Why don't you go home and get some rest. He's sedated, and we can't do any more for him tonight. You need to take care of yourself, Mrs. Flannigan. This will be a long ordeal."

Moira doesn't remember leaving the doctor, the long walk down the hospital corridor, or the flight of stairs that leads to the big double doors. It is only when she feels the chill of the wind and pulls her coat close that she realizes that her neighbor, Mrs. Denison, is beside her to take her home.

The numbness subsides but is quickly replaced by anxiety. Her mind is racing. *How will we survive without Donal's pay check? How can we pay for his care—and food? The children!* "Thank God Michael is twenty-one with a good job!" The words come out of her almost like a prayer, but the sound of her own voice in the chill of the night startles her. *Ellen, sixteen; Christopher, fourteen; and Frank is almost eleven...* Now the tears come in torrents.

Just then the bell at Our Lady's tolls seven o'clock. Moira hears the bell and is comforted. She can't stop crying, and the tears continue to fall until she has no tears left. Mrs. Dennison drops Moira at the front gate to her house. "You need a ride back to the hospital or anything, you just ask."

Their house has been in the Flannigan family for almost one hundred years. It was moved from its original location to Chandler Street when the railroad line was laid along Washington Street. Built by hand, including the windows and doors, everything is out of plumb. There are three bedrooms and a bathroom upstairs; living and dining rooms and a parlor are downstairs, along with the kitchen. It is a cozy home for the whole family. Early on the Flannigans realized how important the land was and

22

planted almost a quarter acre in vegetables. In time they added a grape arbor, a coop for chickens, and a fenced area for a pig.

In the summer of 1938, Donal is able to come home, but everything has changed. Naturally, the children all help with the house and garden, but the family is barely able to make ends meet. Even the atmosphere around them feels different. Michael is responsible; always has been—being the oldest. Ellen is a big help to her mother, not only around the house but in caring for the younger boys. Christopher, the comedian, is ready to enter the tenth grade at Our Lady's Catholic School. He sees life differently. Not with the maturity Michael has, but he manages to find pleasure in most things around him. Frank, the baby of the family, is about to turn twelve. He is neither mature nor comedic, and, unlike the others, he has always had older ones around to do the chores— making it easy for him to avoid work. His favorite subjects are: "Me." and "I'm hungry."

Donal has not adjusted since the accident and keeps more and more to himself. He avoids the family, preferring to eat alone in the front room where a bed has been made up for him and where he spends most his waking hours. Moira understands that he is depressed. Learning to use his right hand for everything when he had been a *lefty* must be frustrating. He lives with back spasms and almost constant pain. He often drops or spills things, and this embarrasses him. He's a proud man used to providing everything for his family, and now his family provides for him. He prefers the solitude, reading, or watching the real world outside the window.

For the past year, the family has learned to live on what they grow in their garden, and they sell the surplus. In winter they use what firewood they can find, or burn peat that comes from the small bog on Hawthorn Street. The children collect coal left on the train tracks running along Washington Street.

"We have to be smart and resourceful," Moira says. "My grandparents emigrated from Ireland during the Irish Potato Famine in 1847, long before I was born. Four million Irish men, women, and children left their homes and settled far and wide hoping for a better way of life." She pours milk into a glass for Frank. "I've seen many changes in the area over the years. I remember when they built the Synagogue down on Adams Street. The Italian families moved in around 1900. Each wave of immigrants brought new languages and new foods, and added another dimension to the neighborhood.

CHAPTER THREE

Approaching the back door of the house, Michael sees his mother struggling with the door and a load of laundry. He puts down the bag of groceries.

"Here, Ma. Let me help you with that."

"What took so long? I expected you back an hour ago."

He follows her to the clothesline strung between two trees behind the house. Michael places the basket on an old weathered stool so she wouldn't have to bend down as much.

"I met Tony down the street, and we talked a while."

Moira reaches into the clothespin bag and pulls out a handful of pins. She puts a couple of pins in her mouth and pegs the pair of trousers on the line before reaching for the next item and pegging it to the line. "What's he up to?"

"He's going to work the carnival the next few nights."

"Michael, don't you go getting any ideas. That daft kid—trouble always finds him, and carnivals fester with trouble! I don't want any of you getting into trouble, hear me?"

"Don't worry, Ma. I have no intention of going there tonight. I've been asked to take the night shift at the mill." He takes two corners of a bed sheet and helps her hang it on the line. The sheets billow in the breeze like sails.

"I love the smell of clean clothes on the line. What time do you have to leave?"

"Not 'til later—right after supper or so."

"Go on with you then. Take a hoe to the weeds around the tomatoes, and pick any ripe ones. I'll slice some up for dinner. Pick some green beans, too. We'll have them for supper." Moira stands for a moment and stretches her back—looking out over the garden. "I reckon the weeds grow better than the vegetables."

"I got dry beans, molasses and brown sugar for baked beans. We haven't had that for a while. I stopped in to Kinchela's on my way home. Ellen insisted I get a newspaper and some tobacco for Dad. She'll be home soon."

"That was thoughtful." Moira reaches for something else to hang. "Poor Donal, he doesn't find much enjoyment these days. Cigarettes seem to calm him."

Michael watches her expression. Ma doesn't find much enjoyment these days either. He sees how she's aged since the accident. Frown lines run deeper and so do the lines around her eyes. But mostly he misses her laughter. She never laughs anymore. He walks to the shed, picks up the hoe, and heads for the tomatoes in the garden.

"Where is that girl?" Moira asks the shirt she's hanging.

Ellen works a few hours a week at a summer job in Kinchela's on the corner of Chapel and Watertown Streets. They sell newspapers, magazines, tobacco; they have a good selection of comic books; and there is a candy counter. This makes Kinchela's a favorite hangout for teens. Neighborhood kids sit on the floor and read the comics until someone kicks them out. The counters are scratched and dented. The wide, wood plank floor is worn and uneven in places, but it shines brightly from the lemon oil Mrs. Kinchela uses to polish it.

"See you tomorrow, Mr. Kinchela!" Ellen calls out, and rushes out the door. In her hurry she almost trips over Tony, who is sitting on the wooden steps outside the door.

"What in heaven's name do you think you're doing, sitting here in everyone's way?" She regains her balance just in time to avoid falling down the steps.

"Hi, Ellen. . . I'm sorry, uh . . . real sorry. I'm just sitting." Tony's face turns crimson as he babbles on. "I didn't mean to... you almost . . . Uh, I'm working at the carnival tonight and tomorrow night, and Michael said he might bring you there . . . tomorrow 'cause he's workin' tonight."

In spite of her annoyance, Ellen restrains a laugh as she watches Tony, usually so high hat and cocky, become all cute and shy. She's known him all her life and feels she can say anything to him. "When are you going to get your hair cut? It's curling down to your collar!" Ellen says, twisting the strap of her purse around her fingers.

His dark eyes grow huge. He's thinking *now he's done it! He's made her mad*—just what he feared. His heart has set on only one girl these last couple years. Ellen. He can't think straight when he sees those light blue eyes. Her long chestnut hair shines in the afternoon light, caught up behind her head with a large blue bow. He knows his heart is lost.

"Tony! Are you listening? You know Ma would never let me go. She doesn't even want the boys to go." Ellen sits down on the step beside Tony. "Ma says they are all lowlife degenerates at the carnival—even if it is at Our Lady's."

"She doesn't have to know, does she? Just say you're goin' to a movie or something. Come on, Ellen. It's a Friday night, geech!" He can't look at her anymore, afraid she'll see the disappointment on his face. He pretends to be interested in a knothole in the wooden steps.

"Tony, why do you use that carnival slang?"

"I don't see what's wrong with it. Lots of guys say it." *Oh no, more criticism.* "What are you going to do when you graduate from high school?" he asks, changing the direction of the conversation.

"I'm going to get a real job. Kinchela's is only for the summer. When school starts, I can still work a little after my classes and on Saturdays. But after graduation I can go anywhere. Maybe even Boston."

"Boston!"

Ellen is proud of her decision. "Oh, yes, Ma says I need to be able to support myself, in case I don't get married straight away."

"Don't go to Boston! I know plenty of guys that would marry you." *Uh oh, I shouldn't have said that! I don't want her thinking about other guys.*

"I've got to go." This conversation is uncomfortable. "I don't know about tomorrow night." Ellen gets to her feet. She takes two steps, turns back, and plants a kiss on his cheek. "See ya!" She quickly walks away.

"What! Oh my God!" *Maybe she does like me.* But I made her mad. She was mad, *wasn't* she?" He watches her go, then straightens up and brushes himself off. Tony stops, smiling as he watches Ellen walk on up Watertown Street heading home.

Arriving home, Ellen rushes in the back door. The family is already seated at the table. "Sorry, am I late?"

"Michael has to work the night shift, so we're eating a bit early. We've said Grace. Wash your hands and come to supper."

Ellen washes at the sink and returns drying her hands with a towel.

"What kept you? Did you work late?" Moira passes the bowl of vegetables. "I needed you to help with the supper."

"I was held up a while at the store," Ellen answers—not wanting Ma to know it was Tony who held her up.

"Take a plate in to your Dad first; then come and eat before your brothers eat it all."

Ellen returns quickly and takes her seat beside her older brother.

"Ma, I've been thinking. School starts next week. Sister Agnes, the principal, has invited some of her business friends to come and talk to the seniors about their future. I want to go and hear about jobs I could get."

"Sister Agnes is a very wise woman. I think you should go."

"Well, there is something else... I mean, my grades are good, and I'm a fast learner, but..."

"What's this on my plate?" Frank asks, looking down at the Boxty. "I think it's smashed. What is this smashed thing?"

"It's a potato pancake. It's supposed to look like that," Michael tells him.

"But I don't like smashed food."

"You like *every* kind of food!" Christopher says.

"Frank, eat it and be still," Moira says, turning back to Ellen. "I can tell you want something."

"Why do I have to eat smashed food?"

"If you don't want it, I'll eat it." Christopher reaches with his fork to take the Boxty, but changes his mind when Moira raises an eyebrow.

"Frank, food doesn't grow on trees, and we can't afford to waste it. Eat." Again she turns to Ellen. "Spit it out, Ellen. What is bothering you?"

"Uch! I 'unt to 'it it out," Frank says. After taking a bite he refuses to chew...

"Spit it out in the waste basket and let me talk to Ellen."

Frank rushes to the waste basket to dispose of the Boxty and returns.

"Christopher, you can have the rest," Moira says.

"Gladly." He makes a show of flying his fork through the air and letting it hover in circles over the morsel. Then, with a dramatic flair, the fork swoops down, impales the Boxty and carries it to his plate. The children laugh, but Moira is annoyed both by Frank and Ellen.

"Ellen?"

Ellen swallows hard before answering. "Ma, this is so important to me. It will be the most important time of my life... my whole life. The changing point... pivotal.. ."

"I hope you get to the point in my lifetime."

"Ma, I need a new dress for this—oh so important— meeting of my life." Ellen's eyes drop to the table fearing the response. "Sister Agnes said we should dress like we were going to an interview. I don't have anything like that."

Frank is getting bored and wants to change the subject. "Ma, why can't we go to the public school? The nuns at Our Lady's are slave drivers."

Moira is losing patience quickly. "I promised God, Frank!" she states firmly, and then tries to soften the sarcasm. "The Sisters of Charity are pious teachers. They may be tough, but you will get a good education with them."

"He's right, Ma. There is very little charity spread in the classroom," Christopher adds.

"Don't start, Christopher. I will not hear a word against those God-fearing women of the cloth. They have given up everything in life just to teach you and Frank." She takes a deep breath and turns once again to Ellen.

"I don't have to tell you things are tight. Besides the bills, your brothers have outworn all their pants and shoes. Maybe later we can find the money."

"But later will be too late! I've saved some money, and the dress I saw is only eight dollars."

"Eight? It might as well be twenty-five!"

"Ellen, I've saved a bit, and I get paid tomorrow. Between us I think we can make it happen. Would that be okay, Ma?" Michael offers.

"I don't see the need. Food and medical bills don't get paid when we squander our money."

"It's not squandering. Honest. This meeting will open the door to a better paying job. Then money won't be so tight. I promise, Ma."

"I can find a bit of extra work for a while. That will help. What do you say, Ma?" Michael asks, thinking about his conversation with Tony.

"Do what you want, Michael. But don't ask for my blessing," Moira answers, getting up from the table and walking out of the room.

Ellen jumps up and hugs Michael fiercely. "Oh, Michael, thank you; thank you! I'll pay you back, I promise. I'll clean the chicken coop for you for a month, if you want. I wish I could show you the dress. It's fabulous. Any time I have a break at work I look at the fashions in Harper's Bazaar and Women's Wear Daily. That's what all the women who work in offices wear." Michael chuckles.

"What about me? Can I get a new shirt for school? All I ever get are Christopher's old stuff that used to belong to you, Michael." Frank scowls, folds his arms roughly, and plops against the chair back.

31

"My pant cuffs are so high everyone thinks they're knickers! My shirt sleeves hardly cover my elbows! I'm the sorriest sot in the 10th grade!"Christopher chimes in.

"You're in the 10th grade?" asks Michael with a grin.

"You know I am."

Michael leans close and whispers, "Then you should go out and get a job and earn your own money."

"What about me? I'm too young for a job. And look, I can't button the top button of this shirt." Frank is the stouter of the two younger boys. He is always the one to finish off food in the bowls. Moira never worries about left-over food with Frank around—except apparently Boxty.

"We'll see what kind of bargains Mr. Fried has to offer; so it's a maybe."

CHAPTER FOUR

They plan to go shopping early the next day when Michael gets home from work. Since it's Saturday, he figures he can sleep later in the day.

"Look, Ellen, why don't we pool our money and see what we have?"

She opens her handbag and turns it upside down on the kitchen table. Two dollar bills and a handful of change tumble out. She counts the coins. "I had a bit more, but I wanted Da to have the newspaper and cigarettes."

"I have $2.49."She smiles with obvious pride. "It took me all summer to save up, but it was worth it."

Michael smiles and reaches in his pocket. He pulls out five $1 bills and counts .51 cents in change. "There you are: $8.00." Fried's should be open by now. Let's get this over so I can get a couple hours sleep."

Fried's shop is only a few minutes away on Dalby Street. Flanking the entrance to Fried's are two display windows with mannequins wearing the latest designs in seasonal colors, and all around them are numerous stylish accessories. Michael cannot imagine what some of them could be used for.

Inside the store are more mannequins, rows of hanging clothes, shelves filled with folded sweaters, shirts and shoes.

"May I help you?" asks Mr. Fried.

"I have an interview for an office job. What would you suggest I wear?"

"Would you prefer a dress or a suit?"

"Dresses please—one I can use on Sunday as well."

"Would you like to try some on?"

"Oh, yes," Ellen says as she looks through the pretty dresses before her.

"You pick a couple out and try them on. Let me know if you need more help," Mr. Fried offers.

Michael is helping Frank and Christopher pick out a shirt each and tries to strike a bargain with Mr. Fried.

Ellen comes out of the dressing room wearing a long-sleeved brown dress with a faux jacket displaying four large brown buttons, and belt. The back and right shoulder have an attached short cape that hangs about half way to the elbow.

"I think I like this one. What do you think?"

"How should I know? I don't think that's a good color for you though," Michael says. Christopher and Frank both make faces, shaking their heads no.

"I think I'd like to try another."

Michael takes a deep breath and pays Mr. Fried for two shirts.

A few minutes later Ellen settles on a cobalt blue dress with broad shoulders and nipped waist; belted—with gold buttons that run all the way down the front to the calf length hem. Beaming and twirling in front of the store mirror she says, "Oh, Michael. This is it! Don't you love it?"

"Oh, good, you're sure?" Ellen nods and returns to the dressing room to change.

At the register Ellen reaches into her purse, pulls out the eight dollars, and hands it to Mr. Fried. "Thanks, Mr. Fried."

Ellen takes the package and hugs it to her chest. "If I could save some money, I could buy shoes. Did you see those over there? I think they match my new outfit."

"Maybe next time," Michael puts his arm around her and guides her steadily out the door. "I'm sure I'm not up to any more shopping for a while."

At home, Ellen changes into the new dress to show Moira. Her reaction is less than enthusiastic, but Ellen isn't daunted. She returns to her room to change again, but with a noticeable spring in her step.

"Don't worry, Ma," says Michael. "It'll be all right; you'll see."

That evening when the family sits down to supper, Ellen talks excitedly about her shopping experience. The boys talk about their new shirts but complain that they still need new trousers.

"Finish up. There are still chores to do," Moira says. "Christopher, the chickens need your attention. Check their food and water before putting them into the coop for the night; the pig gets the leftovers. Michael, would you help get your father washed and ready for bed? Ellen has the dishes to wash up and put away."

Later that evening after things settle down, a thought occurs to Michael for a way to make some extra money.

"Ma, I'm going out for a while. I won't be long." He grabs his hat and coat and heads out the back way. He almost falls over Ellen as he steps out the door. She grabs his jacket and pulls him around the corner, where she knows Ma can't see or hear them.

"Michael, take me to the carnival tonight, please."

"Are you out of your mind? Ma would skin us alive."

"I want to see Tony. He's there working tonight and asked me to come. Michael, please? Can I go, just for a while, not long. It's Saturday night? I see all the lights and hear the sounds. I want to know what it's like at a carnival. I know Ma doesn't want us down there. You can take me and watch over me. I'll tell her I'm going to a friend's house. Pleeeease?"

Michael is a push over, at least when it comes to Ellen and the boys. *Maybe, if I take her to see Tony, and then send her right home, it will be all right.* "Well, I'm going there anyway. I thought I'd see if I could find work. If I can make back the money we spent today, Ma will stop worrying. Go in and talk to Ma. If she asks, tell her you're going to *see* a friend. That way it won't be a lie."

Ellen is thrilled, and hugs him hard.

"I'll take you, but you come home *when I say*. I don't like sneaking around on Ma, Ellen."

"Okay, I promise!" She jumps up and kisses him on the cheek. "I'll do just as you say." She turns and runs into the house.

Michael begins to question the wisdom of taking Ellen to the carnival. He almost hopes that Ma won't let her out. It was bad enough when he was going alone. Ma will be furious if she finds out. He paces nervously, waiting.

Moira is sitting in her rocker with a pile of mending at her feet. She keeps a tight rein on her children because she loves them, and because she's a little afraid. One terrible accident in a family is enough...

The back door opens, and Ellen comes in. "What are your plans for the evening?"

"I thought I might go see a friend, if that's all right. I haven't told anyone about my new dress."

Waiting to hear Ma's response seems to take hours. Ellen is tempted to say more, but she's sure she'll end up telling a lie, or giving away the real reason. Finally Moira stops darning and looks up at her daughter. Ellen holds her breath. Another eternity passes. Moira just looks at her. "All right, but don't stay long. An hour or so, hear me?"

"Thank you, Ma." She gives her a quick kiss on the cheek, grabs her jacket, and runs into the kitchen and out the back door.

"I've got an hour or so," she says pulling Michael to hurry him along.

Once on the street she relaxes as they fall into step. Michael still isn't sure that taking her is a good idea, but he feels it's too late to turn back. They walk down Bottle Alley and cross Watertown Street. He feels Ellen's excitement build as they get closer to Our Lady's and the carnival. The lights, sounds, and smell of popcorn on the evening breeze help him relax. He has a purpose, and he'll focus on that.

Inside the gates they search for Tony. The sights and sounds are a distraction. The music of the merry-go-round and the happy, chattering, festive crowd make it difficult to think. They find Tony manning the Ring Toss booth.

"Oh... hi, Tony, I forgot you were going to be here tonight." Ellen turns and appears to be interested in the Duck Shooting booth across the way.

Michael suddenly sees his sister in a new light. When did she acquire these feminine wiles? *Could this be my little sister, flirting with a boy?* Not just a boy, *Tony!* He watches as they try to hide their feelings for one another. He-man Tony blushes. He struggles for words—ones that won't sound stupid. Ellen is looking everywhere but at Tony. "I have things to do," he interrupts.

"Michael, is it alright if I stay here with Tony for a bit? I want to try this game." Her voice is natural, but her eyes are pleading.

37

"You have one hour, and then it's off to home with you. I'll be back to check. Tony, who do I talk to about getting work? I need to pick up some fast cash."

"Check the last booth in this row; the one on the left. A big Russian by the name of Koslov runs the carnival and does the hiring. It's mostly locals that work the booths."

Tony has not taken his eyes off Ellen all this time, and Michael notices. *Boy, does he have it bad. Ma is going to have a fit when she finds out.*

Leaving the two love birds, Michael makes his way along the booths that line both sides of the wide alleyway. At the end are the Ferris wheel and the carrousel. He sees a bear of a man shouting in what he presumes is Russian. The object of this tirade is a young woman, dressed as a fortune teller, who is yelling back just as loudly in a mix of English and Russian.

"I am *not a prostitute*, and I will not be treated like one! You want a girl to entertain your—so called—friends, you find someone else! You're a right chuccuo!" Furious, she looks for something—anything. Finding a hammer, she hurls it at his head, then storms off, colliding with Michael. She gives him a shove as she passes. She is still raging in broken English, her hands gesturing wildly. Michael watches her go, pushing anyone foolish enough to be in her path. He notices her thin waistline and hears the tinkling of the bells on her costume, hips swaying with each angry step. A heat rises within him as a smile comes to his lips. If he had the time he'd like to follow those swaying hips and get to know their owner a...

"What ju lookin' at, mush?" the big Russian roars. "Ju see somethin' ju like! You stay away from that jival; she not for likes of ju."

"Uh, sorry. . ." Michael is pulled from his reverie. "Are you Koslov? I'm looking for work."

Koslov assesses him. "Maybe ju can work milk bottles, huh? Pukka to the mush I send ju. Tell him to see me. Dummy can't add to save his ass. I lose money every night he works. After he tells ju what to do, ju send him to me. Ju add better than dummy, ju can work till we leave. Bring the takings to me when we close."

Michael finds the booth. The kid appears a couple years older than Ellen, but younger than himself. He doesn't recognize him, so they must not have gone to the same school. But he is young and looking to make money, just like him. The kid has picked up some of the carnival jargon like Tony uses.

"This is my first night. Can you tell me how things work?"

"Simple, the suckers get three balls to throw at the wooden bottles. The bottles are weighted on the bottom and don't fall easily. If they knock all the bottles off the shelf, they get a prize. Three balls for a nickel. You show them how to do it using these bottles. Here, see how light they are? " He hands one to Michael. "Remember—never put the light ones back up on the shelf. Keep telling them how close they came, and get them to keep trying."

"I got it. No problem," says Michael. He feels bad that the kid might lose the job, but he needs the money.

"Any idea what Koslov wants?" the boy asks.

"He said to send you to him."

As he walks off, Michael watches him. *Maybe Koslov will change his mind and give him another job somewhere.*

Before long a young couple stops at the booth.

"Arnie, try this one. Win me a prize." The gum-chewing girl is about seventeen with a whiny, high-pitched voice. The skinny, pimple-faced boy, about her age, shoves his glasses up, jams a fist into his pants pocket, and pulls out some change.

"How much?"

"Three tries for .05 cents."

"Come on, Arnie. You can do it. You got great muscles."

The boy drops two nickels on the counter and takes the three balls Michael offers. The boy shoves his glasses up again. He eyes the bottles closely, takes a step back, and throws the first ball that flies over the tops of the bottles.

"That was good!" squeals the girl in a voice that could shatter glass. "Do it again, Arnie!"

"Stand back, Bertha. I need room to wind up." He eyes the bottles, shakes his arms, presumably to loosen his muscles, steps back, and throws! The ball leaves his hand and sails past Michael—hitting the edge of one of the bottles. The bottle quivers, but doesn't fall.

"One more try! One more try!" she chants. "You can do it! One more try!"

Frustrated, the kid kicks the dirt like a bull in the ring, winds up, and slams the ball so hard his glasses fall off. The ball sails between the bottles and hits the canvas barrier in the back with a loud "whap."

"Aw, Arnie, try again. You almost did it," she whines.

"I can't, Bertha. I think I pulled something with that last pitch. Let's try the merry-go-round. We haven't done that yet." They rush off laughing.

Michael pulls the weathered old watch out of his pocket and checks the time, hoping Ellen has kept her word and is headed home.

A man walks up to his booth wearing a Boston Bees baseball cap. His companion is a young lady who is much younger and clearly not his wife.

"Honey, this is my game. If they knew how good I am, they wouldn't let me play. It doesn't seem fair to take all their prizes."

"Oh, Billy, can you win me one of those pink bears? You know how I love pink," she says with a kind of Southern drawl.

"Sure, Baby, easy as pie. Didn't I try-out at Braves Field the other day? They even said they might call me back. I'll win that pink teddy for you," Billy grabs her around the waist, pulls her to him, and gives her a big kiss, "if that's what you want, Baby." She squeals, whether from surprise or embarrassment, Michael isn't sure. Billy pays his money and takes three balls. He steps back, pauses to wind up, throws the first ball as hard as he can—knocking the top bottle off the stack of three.

"I'm just getting warmed up, Baby." He rolls his shoulders and turns his Bees cap around; another wind up for another throw. Whoosh, goes the ball. It hits the milk bottles with a distinct crack, shakes them, but they don't go down. Billy's face turns red with rage and embarrassment. "I hit those bottles, I know it! This game is rigged! I'll get the cops in here, I swear I will!"

"Look, try again, on me." Michael knows this guy can be trouble, and that is the last thing he wants on his first night. He sets the bottles up again, putting the light bottles on the shelf. "Here you go, try again. You knock 'em down, and the lady gets the teddy bear." Michael hands him three more balls.

Billy winds up again and hurls a fast ball. The light-weight wooden bottles go flying. Billy flexes his shoulders like a player after a rough day. A silent look passes between them. Both know the game is rigged, but Billy has saved face in front of the girl, and he'll let it go.

"You did it! You did it, Billy! I knew you could," she gushes. Michael hands her the pink bear, and she gives it a hug, then turns and soundly kisses Billy. His ego restored, he nods to Michael, and the pair move on up the row.

He is watching them leave when he spots the kid he replaced charging in his direction.

"Koslov fired me!" he yells. "I've worked this carnival for two years, and you got me fired!" He reaches the booth and kicks the wooden counter to make his point. "I'm not going down quietly. Watch your back, mush! I've got friends here!" The kid is still yelling as he storms off, his face beet-red with anger. He picks up a rock and hurls it at Michael. It misses, ricochets off one of the weighted bottles, and falls to the ground.

Ellen comes up just as the kid storms past. "That's Johnny Russo. What's he mad about?"

"I was given his booth, and he got fired."

"He's a real hot head, you know. He got kicked out of Our Lady's in the sixth grade because of his temper. He hangs out with those roughnecks down by the river. I sure hope he's not going to make trouble."

"If he does, I'll handle it. You better get home. Ma will be wondering where you are."

"I'm going now; I just wanted to let you know. Michael, Tony wants to take me to the cinema. You know how Ma feels about him, but I really like him. What am I going to do?"

"Listen, Ellen. I can't keep sneaking around on Ma and helping you and Tony like this. We'll all get caught, and then there'll be hell to pay. "You'll have to solve this on your own. Now go home, please. It's getting late. I'll be home after a while."

"Thanks," Ellen answers, giving him a quick peck on the cheek and hurrying off.

Oh God, why couldn't she fall in love with a nice Irish boy?

CHAPTER FIVE

The air is filled with laughter, music, and the aroma of popcorn and candy apples. The evening passes quickly for Michael as more customers stop to try their hand at knocking over the wooden bottles. He talks several players into taking additional chances, which help to build the take. By the end of the night Michael is exhausted. He closes his booth like his neighbors and follows them to Koslov with the receipts.

Michael stands in line waiting his turn to give the night's cash to the big Russian.

"Did ju count it?" the bear asks without looking up from his tally sheet.

"Yeah," Michael responds.

"Well?" Koslov looks up with a scowl. "Jugonna tell me, or do I gotta guess?"

"Oh, sorry; it's $2.25," Michael says.

"Much better," Koslov says after he recounts it and places the bag of coins in a small strong box.

"Ju come back tomorrow and Monday. We open at one o'clock both days. Ju do as good, and I pay ju 20% of each day's take." I pay on Monday after closing; if ju miss a day, ju get nothing, and don't bother to come back.""

"Deal, Mr. Koslov." He strolls off excited at the prospect of the money. The lights strung around the field beside Our Lady's Catholic Church wink out for the night.

Along Bottle Alley, the warm Indian summer day has turned chill with the night. He spots the woman who had argued with Koslov. She's coming out of a tavern arm in arm with a rough-looking character. She is still wearing her costume of purple and gold, and her large hoop earrings catch the glow from the street lights. She now wears a flowing cloak against the night's chill. The man has dark hair and a beard that makes Michael think he must be another carnival worker. They stagger off towards Our Lady's and the carnival grounds.

She looks up; their eyes meet. She grins, lowers her eyes, whispers something to her companion in Russian, and they hurry away laughing.

Ellen is waiting at the gate to their home. When she looks up, Michael is coming down the road. She runs to meet him, and they walk together. "Oh, Michael, I had such a good time. The carnival is so exciting! Tony got a friend to take the booth for a while so he could show me around. It was wonderful! We talked and talked. He bought me cotton candy. Have you ever had cotton candy? It's like eating sweet cobwebs! I didn't want to leave, but I promised you... and Ma didn't say a word. Can you believe it? I came back out to wait for you."

"I wouldn't get too excited," he says as they reach the back door. "You know she has a way of finding things out. It's kind of spooky how she does it."

Ellen nods her head in agreement. "Remember the time I was skating on the lake and hit that thin spot and fell in? Before I could get home to change my clothes, she knew about it. Mothers must have that third eye they talk about at the carnival. You know the one in the middle of their foreheads?"

"Or, maybe the two in the back of their heads," Michael says, and they chuckle in agreement.

Michael opens the door and goes inside—Ellen at his heels. Moira is sitting at the kitchen table with a cup of tea in her hands and her crochet waiting beside her.

"You're up late, Ma," Michael says, his heart in his toes.

"So did you two have a good time at the carnival tonight?" she asks—not looking up from her crochet.

"Someday I'm going to figure out how you do that," says Michael.

"You never will, because you'll never be a mother. But, for your information, Ellen's clothes smell of cotton candy and popcorn; yours do too. Ellen, go to bed. Michael, your Da would like to talk to you."

Michael knows he's in for it now. Ma usually deals out punishments, at least since the accident. He walks down the hall to the front room.

Donal Flannigan is reading. His glasses have slipped down his nose, and a glass of whiskey sits on the table beside him.

"Sit down, Michael."Donal puts the book down beside the glass. "This is a very good book; *The Yearling* by Marjorie Kinnan Rawlings. One of the benefits of being laid up is I get to read all the time." He takes his glasses off and lays them on the book.

"You did a very foolish thing tonight; taking Ellen to the carnival. Anything could have happened. I understand that you kids want to get out and do things. I can't believe that you and Ellen misled your Ma about where you were going. Ellen is young and foolish, but I expect better from you. What in Heaven's name were you two thinking?" Donal shouts at Michael.

"I'm sorry, Da. She wanted to see what a carnival was like, and I didn't think it would do any harm."

"That's just it Michael, you didn't think."

"I went to get work. They are always hiring. I worked tonight, and I can have the job two more days. They'll leave town after Labor Day. It's a good way to make extra money. I was watching out for her—me and Tony. She was with Tony while I worked, and then she walked home."

"Are you talking about that Italian friend of yours, Pellegrino's boy? I hear tell he's a hooligan!"

"Tony's okay, Da, he's not a bad kid."

Donal picks up his whiskey and takes a sip. As he sets the glass down, it spills. "Dammit!"

"Here, Da. Let me . . ."

"NO! I can do it," Donal shouts and takes out his handkerchief and clumsily wipes the table. But now he's angry. "I'm not sure I want him hanging around our Ellen."

"But we've all been friends for years. Tony has a good side. Maybe that's what Ellen sees."

"She's much too young! Anything could have happened tonight. I can't believe you were so foolish."

"Yeah, I hear, Da." He wishes he had the words to win this argument. "School starts on Tuesday, and then she'll be busy." Michael almost says, 'maybe she'll find another boyfriend,' but catches himself. *That would start something I could never talk my way out of.*

He leaves Da to his reading, happy he wasn't questioned about working at the carnival. He realizes Ma and Da had stayed up late especially to have this talk. Passing through the kitchen, he sees Ma has gone to bed. He hangs his coat and cap on the hook by the door and head up the stairs.

Frank is snoring softly when Michael turns on the light.

"Still got your head, I see." Christopher sits up in bed. "Oh, man, you're in big trouble. I was afraid Da would knock your block off."

Michael sits on the edge of his bed, pulling off his shirt. He unties his shoes, kicks them off, and tosses his socks aside. "Da already talked to me. I was wrong to take Ellen to the carnival, but she really wanted to go, and I didn't see any reason why she shouldn't. But now Da knows about her seeing Tony, and he's not happy. How could I let them suck me into this! Maybe Ellen will lose interest in Tony once school starts." But even as he hears the words spoken, Michael doubts it will happen.

"I can't help you there, big brother. Guess it's one of the hazards of being the oldest." Christopher yawns, turns over, and goes to sleep.

Michael finishes undressing, turns off the light, and lies down. Leaves on the old oak outside dance in the breeze and deflect the glow from the streetlight. He watches the light show on the wall. The dancing specks remind him of the hoop earrings the gypsy girl wore. He replays the scene of her arguing with Koslov, how she stormed off in a rage, and how each step produced a tinkling, musical sound. Her dark eyes flashed in anger as she pushed past him. He remembers her smell and the way she walks. Who is she? What was the argument with Koslov about? Her role must be that of a fortune teller in the carnival; what else could it be? Who was the man she was with leaving the tavern? *Why can't I stop thinking about her!* The sound of a police siren on Watertown Street interrupts his thinking as it moves off into the distance.

CHAPTER SIX

The wind catches a loose shutter, causing a rhythmic tap, tap, tap; and a branch on the maple tree makes scratching sounds. It's the ringing of the phone downstairs that rouses Lieutenant Gillespie, who rolls over in bed and curses under his breath. He shoves his size 9 feet into slippers and rushes out of the room. He pulls the light chain above the stairway, and hopes the ringing phone won't wake his wife or the children.

"Hello," he says, wiping sand from his eyes.

"Sorry to wake you, Lieutenant," says Sergeant Drew from the Washington Street precinct. "There's been an incident down at Our Lady's. The carnival office was broken into and robbed, and that old Russian, Koslov, has been hurt."

"How bad is he?" Gillespie asks.

"There's no word yet. He was found unconscious, and the ambulance took him to Newton-Wellesley."

"Secure the area, and I'll get there as soon as I can."

"We're taking statements from everyone attached to the carnival. Most workers are locals, and they've gone for the night."

"I'm on my way."

Gillespie goes back upstairs and begins dressing.

"Do you have to go?" Clara asks softly.

"There was a robbery at the carnival at Our Lady's. The carnival boss is in the hospital, and they're still checking the damage," he says. He sits beside her and pulls the blanket down. "Maybe I should slip back into bed and keep you warm. He starts to caress her hip and nuzzle Clara's neck.

"Keep that up, and I won't let you leave—robbery or not." Clara closes her eyes, savoring the moment. "I know what's on your mind, Big Boy, and it's not a robbery at the carnival."

"You better believe it," Gillespie slips his hand lower and crawls back in bed.

"You'll be late," Clara says with a giggle.

"I'll use the siren."

In the morning the Flannigan family is gathered at the table for breakfast. Donal has not eaten at the table with the family since the accident, and his presence lets everyone know something has changed. Ellen avoids eye contact—hoping to avert any discussion about last night. Michael is already seated as the other two boys come down the stairs. Frank and Christopher take up their places, and the meal continues in silence as the atmosphere grows heavier. The only sound is the clinking of spoons and forks on the dishware. Moira wipes her mouth on her napkin and breaks the stillness. "Ellen, you will stay home until school starts. You may go to church, but then you come straight home." Moira doesn't look at her. She takes a sip her coffee. "That's your punishment for your behavior and for dragging Michael into it. When school starts, you may go to school, church and work on Saturdays, but that's it until I say different."

"Michael, you're too old to punish that way," Donal says, "but I trust you will not participate in any more deceptions. As the oldest, we expect you to do the right thing. After all, like it or not, you are their role model." A pall settles over the family, and the silence solidifies again. Moira collects Donal's dirty dishes and carries them to the sink. She takes her coat from the hook and walks out the back door. Michael nods to the younger boys to help their Da back to the front room. Christopher and Frank exchange looks. Then they quietly take their empty dishes to the sink and help Donal back to his chair by the front window.

Silent tears stream down Ellen's face. Michael starts to say something, but she holds up a hand to stop him. Any word at all could burst the dam that is restraining her sorrow and rage. She takes the plates to the sink and rinses them before filling the sink with hot soapy water. As the sink fills, she stares out the window. Two squirrels chase each other around the large maple tree in the neighbor's yard. She wonders if she will ever feel that kind of freedom again. Michael comes over with his plate. He hugs her around the shoulders. "It'll be okay. Things have a way of working out."

"I hope so." Her voice is so low he doesn't hear her.

Later, with the table cleared and dishes done, the family walks to church. Donal stays home, of course, too weak to manage the walk or stairs at church. The priest will visit later.

Donal had pressed a few coins into Michael's hand before they left, and said: *After church, go by Mazola's bakery and get a loaf of that Italian bread. I can smell it baking from here. We'll have coffee and a slice of bread with butter and jam when you get back. It will be my treat.* He left his father turning dials on the radio to find a good station.

Nine a.m. mass is out a little after ten, and Mazola's bakery is busy. The family waits outside while Michael stands in line. The smell of bread baking in the brick ovens is making him hungry.

The owners, the Mazolas, had learned the trade growing up in Sicily. Now they make bread for both old and new friends, who cannot resist their fresh-baked breads and other delectable baked goods.

"Michael, how's your papa? I think of him a lot. He used to come into the bakery once a week. I never see him anymore—not since the accident.'"

"He's doing a lot better. He seems to be improving by the day."

"Oh, that's good. You tell him I said hi, okay? Tell him I said I'll bake him something special when he can walk to my bakery again."

"Thank you. I'll tell him."

"Buona giornata, Michael."

"Bye, Mr. Mazola."

CHAPTER SEVEN

The weather is cool, and the leaves are just beginning to turn. Michael doesn't bother buttoning his coat as he makes his way along Bottle Alley heading to the carnival. He likes the change of seasons, and fall has always been his favorite time of year. He thinks of the beautiful gypsy and his step quickens. He has all but forgotten the drama at home when he hears a familiar voice and turns to the sound of running feet.

Hey, Mush! Tony rushes up beside him. "Did ya' hear what happened last night? Ya' must have heard the sirens. Larry Russo was next to me in church and told me."

"No, what? What's up?" Michael's cheerful mood vanishes. After what Da said, he finds himself a little uncomfortable with Tony.

"Someone clobbered Koslov over the head, and stole the money from the safe. It happened right there in his office. Cops were called. Koslov's in the hospital, and they don't know if he'll make it or not."

"What? Do they know who did it?"

"No, but someone saw that fortune teller, Dania, hanging around after closing. She was with that big hulk cousin of hers. Hugo, I think his name is. Those two are always together. Something's very odd about that—don't ya' think?"

53

Dodging traffic, they cross Watertown and continue down Adams Street. "Ya' got any idea who might have done it? That Dania's my guess. She's a right quisterjival, a pretty girl to you, mush. Maybe together with that guy, they robbed the old man and tried to kill him."

"Where do you come up with this rubbish? You're full of bologna... and you sound like a hoodlum! I think you're spending too much time hanging around the carnival."

"What do ya' mean?"

"I heard her give Koslov *what for* yesterday for not respecting her. How could a girl like that do what you said?"

"Well, I just thought. . ."

"And stop going to those Cagney movies. You're beginning to sound like him."

They get to the grounds about 12:30. The area is still quiet, but the crowd will pick up once all the churches let out. Sundays are like that. Michael and Tony walk down the rows of booths to Koslov's trailer.

Two cops stand outside. Tony speaks up first. "Who's in charge? I mean, who's taking Koslov's place? We're here to work the booths."

One of the cops turns and opens the trailer door. "Hey, Lieutenant, you got two mush out here saying they work for the carnival."

Tony turns to Michael and whispers, "I wonder what's going on?" Tony shuffles his feet as they wait nervously for some response.

Michael nudges Tony. "Here he comes."

Gillespie steps out of the trailer and walks over to them. "I'm Lieutenant Gillespie," says the slim; five foot ten police man with a mustache. What he lacks in stature, he makes up for in dignity. He had arrived at the site just as the sun was rising.

54

Sargent Drew had done as he was told and had filled the lieutenant in on the details. Gillespie knows the neighborhood well. He grew up on Pearl Street, just a couple blocks over and had attended Our Lady's School. The Lake is his home, and he guards it fiercely. "You say the two of you work for the carnival?" He studies the young men.

Michael feels like a bug under a microscope; Tony looks like a scared rabbit ready to run. "Yes, Sir, I'm Michael Flannigan. We live up the way, and Koslov gave us jobs running booths for him. We just wondered what booths they want us to cover today."

"You worked here yesterday?"

"Yes, Sir, I came in the evening, and Mr. Koslov sent me to cover the Milk Bottles. You know, throw three balls and knock them over for a prize."

"Yes, Son, I get the idea. How did you do? Make any money at your booth?"

"I guess I did okay. Mr. Koslov told me to come back today and tomorrow."

"And what about you," he asks, turning to Tony.

"Me? Uh, yeah, I worked Friday and Saturday nights." Tony is almost dancing he's so nervous.

"What is your job?"

"I had the RingToss booth uh . . . both nights."

"You boys have any trouble with Koslov or hear of anyone who did?"

"No, Sir," both answer at the same time, but Tony's response is barely a whisper.

"Give the officer your names and addresses, then go see a mush named Tevia in the next trailer." Gillespie speaks to the two police officers. "Be sure to get contact information from everyone coming for work before you send them to Tevia. He heads back

55

to Koslov's trailer muttering, dikkikidotti, as he climbs the couple steps to the trailer. While the door is open, Michael sees Dania. She's been crying, and her hair—*the color of polished mahogany*—falls in ringlets around her face. She looks up and sees Michael just as the door closes.

"That jival is Koslov's daughter. Did ya' know that? Nobody better mess with her. Come on." Tony grabs Michael's arm and pulls him along to the next trailer. They stand outside. Tony, still nervous nudges Michael. "You knock."

Michael raps on the metal door, which makes a hollow, vibrating sound. When he knocks a second time, the door bursts open, and a half-naked man leans out bellowing, "What the hell do you want?"

"Koslov hired us to work the booths." Michael is taken aback by the greeting.

"Yeah, for the rest of the weekend," Tony chimes in, but he steps back behind Michael.

"What do you want me to do about it? I didn't hire you!"

"The officer told us you're in charge of the carnival now," says Michael. "Where do you want us today?"

"Cops, *chuccuo*! Go find Hugo. He's at the Dart and Balloon booth," says Tevia. "He'll fix you up for today. Ask him for a pouch for the change." He leans in so close Michael can smell his breath. "Watch how you make change, mush! No sticky fingers. You get my meaning? Now off with you." With that he slams the door so hard it rattles the whole trailer.

Michael and Tony head back through the aisle of booths toward the back end looking for Hugo.

"If they got robbed last night, how are they going to pay us?" asks Tony.

"I don't know. Maybe they'll pay us from the booth profits."

Up ahead they see a big man with dark hair and beard. Michael stops in his tracks. He is at the Dart and Balloon booth, and it could only be Hugo.

Michael whispers to Tony, "I saw him last night with that girl, Dania. They were coming out of Sullivan's tavern. They seemed very cozy."

"Ya' mean the quista fortune teller, Koslov's daughter?"

"Tony, I really wish you'd speak English!"

"Ya' need to learn a little of the language if ya're going to work around here."

Michael rolls his eyes and moves on. Hugo is talking to a young man. He hands him a pouch, and the boy walks off.

"Hugo? Mr. Tevia said to see you. I worked the Milk Bottle booth last night and wondered if you want me there today and tomorrow, too?"

Hugo eyes Michael. He looks familiar. He knows he's seen him somewhere. He checks his roster. "Take the Cat Rack. He turns, picks up two pouches and hands one to him, before turning to Tony. "What about you?"

"I had the Ring Toss the past two nights."

"Oh yeah, I remember you. Today you get the Hook a Duck. Here you go. Meet me here tonight after closing with the take, and tomorrow check in with me again.

They quickly locate their booths. Tony is across from Michael and two booths down.

"What's the 'cat rack'?"

"It's like the milk bottles but ya' use weighted bags painted to look like cats. They sit on a rack, and the idea is to knock one off with a baseball. I know how it works. I'll show ya' how to control the release."

CHAPTER EIGHT

It's well past 2 p.m., and it's turning into a very long day. Lieutenant Gillespie would like a break, maybe something to eat, and he is thinking of his wife and how the day began...

"Lieutenant Gillespie." Officer Moran has come into the trailer. "The men have finished talking to everyone traveling with the carnival. How do you want us to proceed?"

"Now we talk to the locals working the booths. Miss Koslov couldn't give me any names. Her father might know some of them by name, and Hugo might know the name of one or two."

"The carnival had planned to leave tomorrow night. They have dates booked. They are wondering when we might finish."

"I can't say, but this carnival isn't going anywhere until this business is settled."

"I understand, Sir."

"I'm sorry, I know you're overwhelmed with all this," Gillespie says to Dania as they stand in her private trailer in the *living lot* away from public access.

"Hugo and I must take over his work now that he is in hospital. The carnival winters in Sarasota every year. We play to towns all the way down and back. Some regulars have winter jobs waiting for them. We have to move on." She wipes away the tears that will not stop. She wants to be strong.

"You understand I cannot release you to move for a while."

"We have to be in Sarasota, Florida, by November. What will I do about the towns along the way that are waiting for us? We have made deposits on fair grounds and fields. We'll lose money if we can't make those dates."Dania shakes her head. She bursts into tears, pacing, and screaming oaths in Russian. Gillespie stands helpless. Then, as suddenly as it began, Dania calms herself enough to speak. "I promise you this: before I leave this town whoever did this will be dealt with—your way or mine. I don't care which."

Walking toward her father's office trailer, Dania sees the Cat Rack where Michael is talking to a boy and his date. The boy has not had any luck winning a prize for the girl.

"Try again," says Michael. "I'm sure you can win your friend here a nice prize." Michael secretly works the control releasing a weighted cat. "I have confidence in you. Here, try this one." He points to a lightweight cat on the second shelf.

The boy shakes his head. "I've spent enough money. Come on, we'll try something else."

"Oh, try one more time, Joey. You almost hit one before. Do it again." She smiles up at him.

Joey takes a deep breath ready to insist they leave, but the smile has *please* written all over it. He picks up one of the balls, looks at the target cat, and throws. As the cat falls off the shelf, Joey's mouth drops in surprise, and the girl shrieks with joy.

"What prize would you like, Little Lady?" Jumping up and down, she picks out a pretty doll with long blond hair and wearing a blue gown. She is smiling broadly when Michael hands it to her. She embraces the doll, and without a second thought gives Joey a kiss on the cheek. Color rises in her cheeks as she realizes she has kissed a boy in public.

"Thanks a lot, Mister," says Joey. Now grinning, he takes the girl by the hand, and they move along down the row of game booths.

Dania is touched by the scene. Smiling, she walks away. *Pissa, he's a quister mush.* She thinks.

Michael resets the booth for the next customer, organizing the cats and checking his money pouch. *There is still time for one more player before lights out.* He pulls out his handkerchief and wipes the shelf. When he looks up, he sees Johnny Russo glaring at him, but before Michael can say anything, the kid turns and hurries away. As Michael wonders what the kid is doing here, four teenage boys come up to play. He drops the handkerchief on the shelf figuring he'll finish when they leave.

"Gentlemen, we've got time for a play or two before closing. Are you feeling lucky tonight?"

"Sure am, Mister. I got three nickels and a good right arm. Here's the dough. Now back up, boys, and give the master some room!" The others step back a pace or two. He takes a ball, winds up, throws, and misses.

"Yeah right, you couldn't hit the broad side of a barn if you were standing inside it!" one friend yells. The others laugh.

"You have no faith, my man. Move farther back." He winds up, throws, and misses again.

"Maybe you should let one of the *men* take a turn, *Abercrombie.*"

"Aw, you're all wet," says the third boy.

"Anybody got any money left?" asks the fourth.

"No, I'm beat," says the third.

"Okay. Prepare to be impressed," says the first.

"Hey, look over there!" The second boy points at two girls playing at another booth.

"Wow, I like the looks of them," says the fourth.

"Let's go check 'em out, Pally." All three boys walk off toward the girls, leaving the first boy poised to pitch.

"Hey, wait for me!" The first tosses the ball—almost hitting Michael as he dashes off to catch up with his friends.

Tony signals Michael to wrap it up. It's closing time. Both shut down their booths for the night. Michael counts the take, puts it back in the pouch, and heads for Tony's booth.

""How'd ya' do today?"Tony asks. "Would 'ja give up your job at the mill and do this every day?"

"It was fun, but I don't think I'd like it on a permanent basis."

"Me either. I've been doing some thinking the last couple days. Maybe I should think about trying for a promotion at the mill. A guy has got to grow up sometime."

Michael is stunned by Tony's revelation. *About time* he thinks.

A line has formed at Hugo's. One by one each worker hands over his pouch, tells Hugo the amount collected, and leaves for the night. Hugo is a no-nonsense kind of guy—but not unreasonably gruff; unlike Koslov.

"Good work. See you tomorrow," he says to Michael and Tony, and they walk away.

Hugo continues tallying the day's receipts. He recounts each pouch, checks the tally sheet, and dumps the money into the cash box on the counter.

Dania walks up. "Those two," she says. "What do you know about them? I've seen them around."

"They're late comers that work the booths. They seem good workers. No problems so far," says Hugo.

"Do you know their names?"

"Tony is the dark one; I don't know the other mush."

"I was watching him. He's no green worker." Dania puts her elbows on the counter and rests her head on her hands. "You know, Gillespie won't let us leave. 'Settle things' he said."

"Maybe we will catch him first."

She recoils at this. "Oh, let me catch him first! I'll scratch his eyes out! I'll show that Inga how we deal with scum like him! I'll teach that divia mush not to jawl from us." She grabs a trim knife and slams the blade into the old wooden counter top. It is still vibrating as she turns and walks to the gate.

Tony and Michael walk up Adams Street and stop in front of Sullivan's Tavern. The place is dark inside.

"Darn, I forgot. It's Sunday; the bars aren't open. Guess I'll go home and let my mom yell at me for something," Tony smiles as they continue up Bottle Alley.

"That's fine by me. I'm bushed. I'm going straight to bed when I get home."

"Lieutenant Gillespie stopped by my booth. We have to talk to the cops when we go in tomorrow. I told him I don't know anything about the break-in, but he says they have to question everyone. It's routine, he said."

"I'm not going to worry about that 'til the time comes. I don't have any information for him anyway."

"When he asked if we knew of any trouble Koslov had, you said no."

"So? I don't."

"What about the argument between Koslov and Dania?"

"What about it!"

"Well, you did say she was mad . . ."

"It wasn't anything," Michael says.

"Okay. Geech."

"I'll see you tomorrow."

"Meet me on the corner. Okay?" says Tony. He claps Michael on the shoulder—his way of saying *no hard feelings*. Tony walks on. Michael turns right onto Chandler Street.

Dania speaks to the night security evaluating the added safety precautions that are now in place. Additional men have also been hired.

"Keep your eyes open tonight. No more problems, got it?" Dania heads back to the office. Dania is worried about making the approaching dates, paying locals off tomorrow night. Oh, God, could anything else happen? She finds herself thinking about the man at the Cat Rack. *I saw him when we left the bar last night. I like tall men, and he must be at least six feet. I hadn't noticed his broad shoulders, probably because he wore a coat. But I noticed today when he was working with that young couple. He's not Italian, or Jewish. He might be Irish with that sandy hair.* "What's the matter with me? I don't have time for this!" She walks a little faster, but like gum on a shoe, thoughts of him stick. *I wonder what his story is. Working the carnival? A guy like that would have a good paying job, in an office probably. Does he have a wife, maybe, and a family to support? Could be he needs more money?* "Why do I care?" *What is it about him? I want to know better . . .*

Rain is starting to fall gently when Michael opens the back door and steps into the warm kitchen. He hangs up his coat and cap and goes upstairs to his room and begins to undress. He realizes he left his handkerchief at the booth. *I'll get it tomorrow if it's still there. No great loss if it's not.*

"Have they caught the guy that robbed the carnival?" Christopher asks.

"Not yet. They're still talking to people."

"Do you think they'll be talking to you?" Frank sits up in bed, obviously fascinated that his brother is involved in an actual crime.

"I don't know. Go back to sleep." Michael finishes undressing and climbs into bed. The young boy groans and turns over. Michael is exhausted, but thoughts of Dania, the carnival, and Lieutenant Gillespie run through his mind. It feels like hours before he finally drifts off.

CHAPTER NINE

Michael is sound asleep when the rooster crows. *If we didn't need that darn rooster, I swear I'd kill it.* Michael pulls the covers over his head hoping for a few more minutes. Sometime later the clatter of dishes wakes him. He looks over and sees the other beds are empty. He dresses quickly and heads down to the kitchen.

Moira dishes oatmeal from the big iron pot. Ellen is still sulking as she brings a plate of buttered toast to the table. Donal sits at the head of the table talking to Christopher and Frank about Sunday's Boston Bee's baseball game. They had listened to it together on the radio and now are very animated as they review the various plays they feel were poorly called.

Donal is happy again, and things are beginning to feel more like the old days. His depression after the accident was ominous, and they worried it might become permanent. But something has changed to bring him out of it. He is even moving around the house more; even following the exercises the doctor gave him.

Moira watches Donal as he entertains the children with stories from his childhood at school. "One of the rules when I was about your age, Frank, was to bring in firewood. We burned it in a stove that warmed the whole room."

"That would be fun! I would like to do that." Frank takes a big bite of his oatmeal.

"We were expected to straighten the desks, sweep, and dust the room, too."

"No, Sir!" Christopher scowls. "That's woman's work!"

"Work does not have a gender. Everyone pitches in to get all the work done," Ma says before taking a bite of toast.

"What else did they do in the old days, Da?" Frank asks with his mouth full.

Ellen finally joins the conversation. "Ma, how did you meet Da, and how old were you when you got married?"

Moira smiles at the memory. "More coffee, Donal?" He shakes his head; he's getting full. "We met at a dance. I was about 18, I guess. We got married when I was about 22."

"Eighteen! You were a year older than me when you met the man you married?" She begins to tear up. "It's just not fair!" She tosses her spoon down, sending oatmeal flying. She leaves the table, and dashes upstairs to her room.

"Oh, my, what was that all about?" asks Donal.

"It's a girl thing; nothing to worry about." Moira calmly takes a sip of coffee. She understands the reason for the sulking. She's pretty sure it has to do with Tony, and she's confident that it will all blow over in time.

"I'd like to sit outside for a while. Michael, will you help me?" Donal asks.

Michael is surprised. This will be the first time he's been out since the accident, and what a wonderful surprise it is. "I'd be happy to, Da."

"I'll help, too." Christopher says pushing back from the table. "I'll get the rocker."

"I'll get . . . uh, I'll get a blanket." Frank leaves the table and runs out of the room.

The boys help Donal out the back door and get him settled comfortably under the apple tree. From here he can watch any cars that go by and anyone walking on the sidewalk in front of the house. Moira asks Christopher to bring a chair from the kitchen. She grabs her shawl and a bowl of peas to shell while she sits.

"Okay, Ol' Man, what are you up to? A week ago you seemed ready for the grave, and now you decide to rejoin the world? What's going on in that head of yours?"

"Well...," he takes a deep breath and lets it out, giving himself time to form an answer. "It's Ellen and that Italian of hers," Donal says gruffly.

"She's not a little girl any more...and I want to go to her graduation. She is seventeen and very pretty. What if she decides to get married? How would it look if a hobbling ol' cripple walked her down the aisle?" he sighs. "I was feeling so sorry for myself that I forgot about the things I love. My kids still need me. Michael is working at the mill and the carnival... working two jobs because of me. The kids do all the chores I used to do. They don't complain; they even seem to enjoy it." He adjusts the blanket and turns toward her.

"When I had the talk with Michael the other night, I learned that Ellen had gone to the Carnival to see Tony. It made me realize that they're all growing up, and how much I was missing by just sitting in that chair.. . I watched the world go by outside and didn't realize *my* world is *inside*. I still have my family. One day they'll leave, but for now I have them. I'm their father, and I'd better start acting like one again. They used to talk to me about school and what they were doing with their friends. I want that again. I miss being with everyone."

Moira keeps shelling peas, letting Donal talk.

"I've not been fair to you, either," he continues. "I made myself an invalid and wallowed in it. I convinced myself I was useless. Dr. Stephens tried to talk to me. He told me I could get back on my feet, but I wouldn't listen. Moira, I'm so sorry."

"Donal, I know how hard it is for you to admit all this," Moira says reaching for his hand. We still need you around here, and if Ellen runs off with that Italian, I'll kill her. You can help."

They sit back still holding hands. A long silence passes. They sit under the tree as the wind picks up and storm clouds form across the morning sky.

The rain passes quickly, and the sun comes out again. Michael meets Tony as planned, and they head down Adams Street to the carnival grounds. Tony prattles on about what questions the police might ask, but Michael's mind is on Dania— her mahogany-colored hair, her eyes that can go from gentle pools of dark chocolate to brimstone and fire in an instant, and how he wants to know her better.

Tony suddenly snaps his fingers in front of Michael's face. "Hello, anybody in there?"

"What? I'm listening. Don't worry. They'll ask questions, and we'll answer what we can. That's all there is to it. Relax."

The police are at the gate checking everyone who enters. Some are directed to Hugo's booth, and those who weren't interrogated before are directed to the office to speak to Lieutenant Gillespie. Officer Moran takes their names, addresses, phone numbers, and license plate numbers if they have a car, and asks them to wait outside until they're called.

They are sitting outside the office trailer when Dania passes. She glances briefly in Michael's direction. Just then Gillespie calls him inside. The office is small and cramped. Gillespie is shuffling through papers on an old desk. He finds

Michael's name on one of them and looks up. "So how long have you been working for Koslov?"

"Saturday was my first time," Michael answers nervously.

"Do you have a regular job?"

"I work full time at the Aetna mill."

"Ever been in trouble, Michael?" asks Gillespie tipping his chair back.

"No. Never."

"At this point everyone is a suspect. I'll be checking police records, and if you're not telling me the truth, I'll find out. Why are you working at the carnival if you have a job?"

"My father is out of work, and the family needs the extra money. The younger kids needed clothes for school. I got what I could with my pay and need to make it up."

"So robbing the carnival would solve your money problems right?"

"I didn't do it. Tony Pellegrino and I walked home together. I stayed home all night. You can ask my brothers. We share a bedroom. I didn't know anything about the robbery until Tony told me after church."

"Did you see anyone else around on your way home?" Gillespie sat up in the chair. Taking a few notes as Michael spoke.

"I did see the fortune teller, Dania, and the big guy, Hugo, coming out of Sullivan's. I know they saw me, too."

"OK, you can go. We'll contact you if we need anything else."Michael gets up and heads out.

"Moran, send Tony Pellegrino in here."

While Tony is in the office, Michael looks for Dania. He has no idea what he will say if he finds her, but he weaves his way around the trailers and down the rows of booths. He spots the fortune teller's tent and heads in that direction.

Inside is a small table covered with a large scarf edged with four-inch fringe that reaches the floor. Dania is dealing out Tarot cards to herself.

Michael smiles and says aloud: "I wonder if any of this stuff *really* works?"

"It depends on who uses them."Dania says putting the deck down. "What are you doing here? Don't you have work to do?"

"Uh, I'm Michael Flannigan. I just wanted to say how sorry I am about your father. Have you heard how he's doing?"

Dania eyes him closely. His sandy hair is windblown, and a strand falls on his forehead. As though he's reading her thoughts, his hand quickly brushes the unruly hair away. "Thank you for your concern. I went to see him this morning. He's awake and talking a little. I spoke with him a bit, and then he talked with Hugo."

"I'm sorry; it must be hard for you, taking over the carnival and all."

"I thought I might, at first. But Hugo will probably take the carnival. God forbid—a daughter—a *female*... It's. . . It's a sore subject."Dania takes a cleansing breath and continues. "Hugo is his choice, even though Hugo is dumb as an ox. He's still better than a *woman!*"

"I . . . uh, it's none of my business but why . . ."

"In my culture, women do not run businesses or make business decisions. That is the man's job."

"Work has no gender," Michael says, and she smiles.

"We're anxious to get on the road."

"I'd better get to work." He pauses. "Dania, if you need to talk, I'm here," Michael says taking her hand. They both feel electricity in the touch. Dania hesitates, and then quickly pulls her hand away. He turns and walks out of the tent. He is half way up the row of booths when Dania calls him. "Michael!" He turns back. "Thank you," she says, and disappears into the shadow of the tent with a flash of purple and gold, and the tinkle of her jewelry.

CHAPTER TEN

Michael is assigned the Cat Rack booth again. He finds he actually likes working at the carnival. He is good at the banter and getting people to take extra throws at the stuffed cats. He is also getting better at enticing strangers to try for the first time. He knows a lot of the crowd from the mill, school, and the neighborhood. Starting up a good chat usually gets them to try. A few times he lets someone win so they will have a prize to carry around. He feels that it's good advertising, and it creates repeat business. When things are quiet, he hunts for the handkerchief he lost, but he doesn't find it.

Michael sees Hugo coming his way. He walks like a man with a purpose, and the scowl on his face is not a good sign.

"Michael, we have a problem. Lieutenant Gillespie says we can't leave before Saturday. We can only run the carnival in the evenings because the kids are in school now. Can you work the next few nights until they let us leave?"

"I can do it," Michael says. He needs the money, but he also wants the chance to stay close to Dania. Michael's thoughts are racing. *I don't want the carnival to leave. After talking to her... I need to ask her out. Would she go? I'll never see her again if she leaves.*

Now time seems to drag. Michael watches for Dania all day, but he doesn't see her. There are many people who come to play, and he tries to stay focused. His thoughts keep returning to Dania, though, and her last words to him: *Michael! Thank you.*

Finally, the crowd thins out, and the carnies prepare to close for the night. Michael tallies the take and heads to turn his money in.

"How'd you do?" Hugo asks companionably.

"Eight dollars and thirty cents—my best yet," Michael says.

"Good. Holidays are the best." Hugo takes the pouch from Michael. He counts out dollar bills, some change, and hands it to Michael. "Here is your pay for the evening and the two days you worked."

"Thank you," Michael says. "I'll be back about 3:30 tomorrow." Hugo is already working with the next vendor.

"How'd ya' do?" asks Tony, as they meet at the gate.

"Not bad. How about you?"

"I made $5.26. It'd have been more, but the cops being there loused up the Sunday sales."

"I'm happy with what I got. I wasn't expecting a windfall, but it's still good. They've asked me to come back tomorrow and work 'til they leave."

"How can ya'?"

"What? Work two jobs?" Michael takes a deep breath. "It's only evenings 'til the end of the week. I can handle it." He doesn't tell Tony that the real reason is Dania.

"I wonder if I should try to do that, too. I could use the extra money." Tony says good night and runs back to the Dart and Balloon booth to speak to Hugo.

In spite of his fatigue, Michael's thoughts keep him awake for a while. But eventually sleep comes, and all too soon it is time to get up again. Today will be the first of his double-shift venture.

The thought of seeing Dania brings him out of bed, and he quickly dresses.

He is coming down the stairs when Christopher and Frank burst in the door and run to the kitchen.

"They found... a dead body... down by the lake." Christopher and Frank have run all the way and are gasping for breath.

"Who's dead?" Moira asks, refilling Donal's coffee cup.

"We don't know yet," Christopher says breathlessly.

"We saw a commotion... and went to see what was going on." Frank bends over with his hands on his knees in an effort to catch his breath.

"Danny Fitzsimmons was there," Christopher says. "He said they had found a dead body. . ." he takes a deep breath, "floating in the lake. He said the hands were tied with a handkerchief. The person was killed and dumped there."

"Never mind dead bodies."Moira gives them a stern look. "And why in the name of all that's holy aren't you on your way to school?"

"But Ma . . .," Frank begins.

"You will find out more about it later—after school." She calls toward the stairs, "Ellen! Get a move on! No point being late on your first day back."

The boys grumble but turn to go back the way they came. Frank snatches a piece of toast as he passes the table.

Ellen comes down wearing her new dress. "What do you think? Do I look like a real working girl?" She does a quick twirl to demonstrate. "I'm so excited; I couldn't eat a bite, Ma."

"No, you don't, young lady. You cannot go to school without some breakfast." Moira gestures to her seat at the table.

Ellen takes a gulp of her coffee, grabs the last piece of toast, gives Ma a quick kiss, and dances out the door.

Michael hasn't been listening. He's thinking about the news they just heard. "They didn't say whether the body is a man or a woman."

"No," Donal says taking a sip of coffee. "It's probably some hobo."

"Or maybe one of those hooligans with that carnival," Moira adds.

Michael is shook by this remark, and suddenly he has to get out of there. "I'll be late for work." He takes his dishes to the sink, kisses Ma, and leaves.

"First, it's Ellen, then Michael. Whatever happened to eating breakfast together?"

"They're growing up, that's all," Donal shrugs. He takes another sip of coffee and glances at Moira over his cup. "She was pretty in her new dress, wasn't she? She'll be driving all the boys mad this year. When did she get so pretty, and so grown up?"

"As they grow older, so do we. It's all God's plan—whether we like it or not. It's such a nice day. Would you want to try walking a bit? The doctor comes this afternoon, and you can tell him how well you're doing. Maybe we'll pick up some news of that dead body."

It is the idea of a dead body that gets Donal moving. The young kids left for school leaving their parents to get all the gruesome details. Donal is not too steady on his feet, so he holds onto Mrs. Fitzsimmon's fence with one hand and uses his good hand to manage his cane.

Mrs. Fitzsimmons calls to them from her porch, "Moira, why don't you and Donal come and rest a minute on the porch?"

"Why, thank you, Caddie." Donal's breathing is labored, but he pushes himself to climb the four steps up to the porch.

"It's usually so quiet with my mister gone. It helps me fill the time to chat with whoever passes."

"We appreciate your offer. Donal is building his strength. The bit of rest will do him good. We'll just stay a minute and then be off," says Moira as she helps him take a seat and sits beside him.

Caddie Fitzsimmons leans forward excitedly in her chair. "I learn all the goings on around the lake. I have a good view being on the corner like this. Usually it's just a bunch of noisy kids that bring the police, but, oh my, all this excitement!" She moves to the edge of her seat.

"It started during the night, or maybe just before dawn. At any rate, when I woke this morning, it was still dark, and there were flashing lights everywhere. They lit up the whole neighborhood: police cars, ambulance, fire trucks. Apparently, someone was walking by.. . I can't imagine who would be strolling at that hour, but, you know, as we get older we don't sleep as well. Well, whoever it was saw something floating near the bank. They started to pull it out and, oh Lordy, realized what it was and called the police.

"I wouldn't go over there. I didn't want to be in the way, but Mrs. Jarvis said it was a body. Boy or girl, she didn't know, but she said the hands were tied, so you know that wasn't any accident. Later, I heard it was the body of a local boy."

"Do they know who it is yet?" asks Donal.

"They think it was Johnny Russo. The police went to get his mother to identify him. I can't believe they'd bring that poor woman all the way down here 'til they are sure it's him." She pulls a handkerchief from her pocket and blows her nose.

"They brought the body up from the lake. Onlookers were all standing around, but they parted to let them through. Johnny

Russo's mother walked with her head down beside the stretcher carrying her son. The neighbors patted her on the shoulder as she passed and expressed their condolences, but I don't think she heard any of them." She sniffles and blows again. "That poor woman."

"We'd better go. Thank you, Caddy." Donal struggles to his feet, and Moira helps him down the steps to the walk.

"Yes, thank you, Caddie," Moira says as she turns to Donal. "You doing ok, Donal?"

"I'm fine. It's just all this excitement, dear. I couldn't stay any longer," Donal says to Moira. "That Russo boy went to school with our children."

They make their way slowly. Moira has her arm around Donal's waist to support him as he manages his cane.

When they get home, Donal collapses on a kitchen chair.

"I'll fix some hot tea with some bread and jam while you get your strength back," Moira says. "Later we'll go to the front room where you can rest until the doctor gets here."

"I did it, Moira," Donal says.

"Did what? Kill Johnny Russo?" Moira asks, confused. She has her back to him, filling the tea kettle at the sink.

"No, you silly goose, I walked to the corner and back. I used to think I'd never walk again. But I did, and I feel great! Well, my back hurts, and I'm exhausted, but I really feel good about today!"

Moira puts the kettle on the stove to heat and goes to Donal. She kisses him on the top of the head. "You did wonderful today, and I'm so glad you didn't kill Johnny Russo," she giggles.

CHAPTER ELEVEN

Dark clouds approach. In a small town news travels fast, and something like finding a body in the lake tops the list.

Rain begins to fall as Michael clocks in. He waves to Dave.

"You hear what happened?" Dave asks.

"You mean the body in the lake?" Michael asks. He holds his breath as he takes off his coat and hat. "Who was it? Do you know?"

"Yeah, that hot head, Russo. You know him?"

"What! Johnny Russo! Are you sure?"

"The police were at the lake when I came to work. Man, we haven't had anything like this in twenty years, and now two things in less than a week." Dave walks off, and Michael carries the coat and hat to the cloak room and hangs them up.

Thank you, Lord. It wasn't Dania.

Michael works quietly the rest of the day, waiting for the whistle to blow.

Michael dodges puddles on the walk home from the mill. He eats a bite, changes, and is leaving for the carnival when Ellen grabs him outside the back door.

"Michael, I need your help. Would you get a message to Tony for me?"

"Oh no, we are not doing this again!" Michael says.

"Please," Ellen's eyes are pleading. "When you see him, just ask him if he wants to see me again and tell him I'm working at Kinchela's on Saturday. I get off at one."

"Ellen, what are you thinking? You're grounded and still finding ways to make things worse."

"Michael, pleeease."

"I wish I could. I'd do almost anything to make you happy, but this is. . ."

"I like him, Michael, and he likes me. He's not what they think; he's sweet and shy. He just puts on an act. You know him. He's really good inside."

"Yes, I guess so. He needs to grow up. That's for sure. He needs to take things more seriously." Ellen's eyes grow sad. Michael sighs, "Especially if he wants to see my sister."

"Then you'll do it?" Ellen starts to give him a hug, but he stops her. Michael shakes his head. "I love you with all my heart, Ellen, but I can't always be there for you. Ma is already mad at us. You and Tony will have to work this out on your own."

The carnival grounds are muddy from the earlier rain. Walking through the gate, Michael hears people talking about Johnny Russo. There are uniformed police walking among the sparse late-afternoon crowd. It's a work night, and not many people are there. *Most probably they've spent what they could afford on the weekend. If they come now, it's from curiosity over this latest trouble.*

He passes the open door of the office trailer. Lieutenant Gillespie is there again asking questions. He sees Hugo sitting on an old chair. Hugo looks defiant, and is arguing with Gillespie. Michael needs his cash pouch, so he knocks on the door frame.

Gillespie looks up. "What do you want?" he asks roughly.

"Sorry to interrupt, but I need my assignment and pouch for tonight."

"The carnival is shutting down, but you stay there. I want to talk to you."

Michael's stomach does a flip. *What could the Lieutenant possible want with me?*

Just then Hugo leaves in a rage and slams into Michael, almost knocking him down. "Out of my way, Mush!" Hugo elbows past.

Lieutenant Gillespie calls Michael inside.

"Have a seat," he says, indicating the chair Hugo had occupied.

Gillespie sifts through some papers before looking at Michael. Finally, he lays them on the desk and settles back in his chair. "Michael Flannigan, right? And you live here in The Lake?"

"Yes, just past Watertown on Chandler Street."

"Did you know Johnny Russo?" Gillespie asks.

"I know who he is. We went to the same school, but I was ahead of him. We didn't hang around together or anything." Michael is uncomfortable.

"Was there any trouble between you and Russo?"

"No not really. Like I told you, Koslov had me take his booth last Saturday night."

"Well, you get to tell me again, Son." Gillespie's tone has changed, and he moves forward in his chair.

"Koslov called him a dummy. He was angry about the money."

"You and Russo? Were any words exchanged over it?"

"On his way out, Russo passed the booth where I was. He was mad about being let go. He yelled at me, but it wasn't an argument."

"Did you see him at all after that night?"

"I saw him one other night. He walked past the booth. He was pushing through the crowd, and he looked really angry about something." Gillespie's eyes narrow, making Michael wonder if he is in trouble.

There is a long silence as Gillespie sits back in his chair. He studies Michael for what feels like a very long time. Then he picks up the papers. "Okay, you can go now," Gillespie says, making notes on the papers.

Michael is relieved to be out of that stuffy office. He realizes he's been sweating. Maybe he should go home, but he hasn't forgotten Dania and goes to look for her.

As he walks down the row, he sees carnies dismantling the booths. One crew is breaking down the rides; others are pulling up tent stakes, packing all the games of chance, and getting ready to move on. There are a number of official-looking people working in a cordoned-off area. With each step Michael becomes more anxious. What he sees next stops him cold. They are taking down Dania's tent! He rushes over. Maybe they will tell him where she is.

"Excuse me," he says to three brutes pulling up stakes and working the lines. "Can you tell me where..." He is interrupted by shouting behind a tarp.

"Don't you dare drag that in the mud, *Chuccuo*!"Dania is standing, hands on her hips, and giving orders to the men. "You, there! Be careful with that. It's older than your family tree! And you...pack those bits and pieces carefully in the carton. I don't want them rolling into one another and breaking." She sees the three men are ready to collapse the structure. "Hold on, we're not ready here," and to the others, "You! Work faster!"

Michael watches with mixed feelings. He's thrilled to see her alive, but it's obvious she'll be leaving town soon. For the first time he sees her dressed in regular clothes. Her brown trousers are tucked into her boots, and the green jacket over her cream sweater accentuates her figure. Her hair hangs in damp ringlets from the light mist that is falling again. Carnival lights dance in the puddles around her feet. Michael is captivated.

Dania sees him, cocks her head, and raises her eyebrows. "And what are you looking at, Mush?" she asks with a grin.

"I was enjoying the most beautiful sight I have ever seen."

"A tent torn down is beautiful to you?" She knows exactly what he means but likes to play.

Without thinking, Michael walks over and takes her in his arms. Her eyes flash. She starts to say something, but his lips are on hers before she can utter a word. "You are fascinating," he whispers a moment later. His lips meet hers again. Her lips part, just a little. He feels her hands on his chest... Then she pushes him away. Breathless and blushing, she turns. She has gotten more than she bargained for with her game.

She turns and looks over her shoulder at him. "We need to talk, away from people with big ears." She turns to the men, "Get on with your work."

Michael follows her behind the tent to the trailers.

"This is home to carnival people. You just see a mix of sizes and shapes, and probably think a half-dozen are ready to fall apart. But we are busy elsewhere most the time.

Michael notices that the office trailer is the biggest and sits well away from the others.

"Come inside out of the rain," she says. Her trailer looks fairly new. She goes up the steps, unlocks the door, and they enter.

"Sit down," she says, nodding to the small eating area. "Would you like coffee?"

"If it's not too much trouble," Michael answers—slipping into the bench seat at the table. It's a tight fit for his frame. He watches as she takes off her wet jacket and toes her boots off. She fills the coffee pot with water and coffee and places it on the stove.

The trailer is small but neat. The paneled walls and domed ceiling are wood. The roof is low, but he can stand up straight. It's compact, and every inch has a purpose.

"I'm not sure what's going on here, Michael," Dania says in her intriguing Russian accent, as she sits down opposite him. "I like you. How much I don't know." She looks into his blue eyes and continues. "We come from different worlds, and soon I will be moving on. This is the life I know." The coffee pot is percolating in time with Michael's heart beat. "We came from Russia, my father, Hugo and I. My mother died many years ago. We were with the circus then, but the war came, and things were never the same. We left."

She absently picks up a carnival flyer on the table. "My father had a knife act and thought he could join a circus here." She aimlessly tears the flier as she talks. "He got an offer to buy the carnival, and that is what he did. It is not an easy life, and sometimes I wish I could leave. My father and I fight about this sometimes, but I give in and stay... telling fortunes; telling them what they want to hear. You will find money or a great love. Too bad I cannot tell my own fortune. Then I'd know what to do."

Michael puts his hands over hers. How delicate her fingers are. "I don't have any answers. All I know is that I would like time to get to know you." She smiles and squeezes his hand. "When do you leave?" She begins to tear up and looks away.

"And one more question, what in heaven's name is a mush? I have been called that ever since my first day here?" This makes her laugh.

"We will leave when the police say we can. They have not found who broke in and hurt my father, and now that poor boy is dead." She forces a smile. "Mush, is our word for a guy."

"Oh, good. I was thinking the worst."

"No, it's ok. Many of the carnival workers are from Eastern Europe, Russia, Romania. It is a language that unites us all. Your young men are picking it up. I have heard them. They use it among themselves as a code only they know."

"Do you have to leave with the carnival? Could you stay a while?"

"How can I do that? How would I support myself? Should I be a prostitute on the streets for my supper?"

She gets up and pulls cups from the cupboard. She puts milk and sugar on the table, and goes for the steaming coffee.

"What makes you say that?"

"My father wants me to entertain his friends—politicians he needs to get the permits. What he doesn't know is how they grab and make remarks when he is not looking. Their hands on me... The smell of their cigars makes me sick." She looks away for a moment. "I will choose who I make love with! No one makes me or chooses for me!"

Michael is charmed by her bit of a temper. No one else he knows does that, and he likes her spirit. *Maybe Ma would too. But if she leaves, she will never meet Ma or the family.*

"Do the police suspect anyone? Lieutenant Gillespie talked to me again tonight."

"He has talked to me again, too." She takes a sip of coffee. "They found a tent peg with blood on it in Silver Lake. He thinks it was someone from the carnival that killed Johnny Russo."

Michael thinks about this as he drinks the strong hot coffee.

They talk for a while about the robbery and Johnny Russo. They talk about where the carnival will go from here, and Dania's life on the road. It is getting late. Michael has to pull himself away.

87

They stand at the door—not wanting to say goodbye. He kisses her one more time before he leaves.

CHAPTER TWELVE

Later that evening, Ellen is sitting on her front porch with Tony. The young couple sits under the porch light as the drizzling rain continues. Few people are on the street at this hour.

"I 'm glad I asked Ma if I could see you. She called your mother, and they had a long chat about us. That's why your mother sent you over." Ellen knows her father is in the front room listening and watching. Ellen understands that this is a test.

"How were things at work?" she asks.

"Good, good,'" replies Tony. He's nervous, knowing this was a breakthrough for them. Her parents were never cordial in the past. "How was school?"

"Good, good." They exchange glances, grateful to have the time together.

"Oh, look, that's Michael coming," says Tony, tipping his chin toward the street. "Wonder why he's not working tonight?"

"Hey, you two, did the earth stop spinning or something? I take it Ma and Da know you're out here." Michael comes onto the porch, out of the rain, and leans against the railing.

"Yes, they know. I asked, and they said it's alright." Ellen signals with a glance at the front room window as if to say, Da is watching. Michael gets it.

"I guess they think it's better here, where they can watch, than off somewhere doing God knows what," Michael whispers. "You know they care about you—both of you, and your reputations. They're only strict because they love you, Ellen."

"Nothing would happen, Michael. We like each other; that's all." Tony winks at Ellen.

Ellen hears her father's chair creak and asks quickly, "Why are you home so early?"

Michael sits on the porch railing. "They closed the carnival, but the police still won't let them leave for a few days. That Lieutenant Gillespie thinks someone from the carnival is responsible for Johnny Russo's death."

"I knew Johnny, and he had a temper. His mouth would engage before his brain had time to think," Tony says. "He worked at the carnival every year. I imagine he was furious when you took his spot."

"He was. He told me to watch my back, and he blamed me for losing his job. I saw him another night. He didn't say anything to me then, but he was obviously mad about something."

The front door opens, and Donal is in the doorway. "Mind if I join the party?"

"Sure, Da," Michael says. Tony gets up and holds the screen door open while Michael helps the older man down the single step to the porch and guides him to a chair.

"I heard you talking about that Russo kid and the carnival. An old man gets hungry for news when he's stuck inside all the time." He gets comfortable. "So, they think it was someone from the carnival?"

"I was talking with a girl there named Dania.

"You talked to Dania? Finally," Tony exclaims.

"Tony," Michael cautions, and turns to his father. "She's the owner's daughter. She told me the police found a tent peg by

90

the lake with Johnny's blood on it. That's how they are connecting it to the carnival."

"Do you think he might have had a run in with someone from the carnival, maybe over losing his job?" Donal asks.

"It is possible," says Michael.

"Well, it's getting late. Ellen has school, and you two have work tomorrow," says Donal, looking at Tony. Best we all should be on our way.

"Would it be all right if I walk Tony to the corner, Da?" Ellen asks.

"Yes, but then come straight back. No lollygagging. We don't want to get the neighbors talking."

Tony and Ellen bounce out of their chairs, dance down the stairs, and down the path to the road. They lock hands and stroll to the corner of the road, taking as much time as they can.

"There'll be a wedding here someday," Donal laughs.

"That wouldn't be so bad. Would it, Da?" Michael is not thinking of Tony and Ellen.

CHAPTER THIRTEEN

"We have to get back to Florida or lose the winter money!" Hugo roars.

"It ain't my fault them cops are stoppin' us," Tevia shouts back.

Hugo paces in the small office. "Dania is driving me crazy," he says. "She keeps asking me why Koslov wanted to speak to me. He's coming home tomorrow. What if he tells her? What if she goes to the police? She might do that just so the carnival can move on."

"She worries about the people who work the carnival year 'round," Tevia explains. "You can't blame her for that. People need to eat, Hugo. They need to survive; she needs to survive, too."

Tevia gets up, opens the small fridge, takes out two bottles of beer, and hands one to Hugo.

"I've seen her talking to that mush. What's his name, the Irish one? Michael, that's the one," Hugo says. He is calming down and takes the old battered chair facing Tevia.

"I got an idea," Hugo says.

"I ain't goin' to like this, am I?" asks Tevia cautiously.

Hugo moves to the edge of his seat. He lets the plan form in his mind as he talks. Hugo may not be as stupid as Dania thinks, and he never knows who might be listening. He leans close and whispers, "What if we get the police to believe Dania and this Michael killed Russo?"

"Why would they kill Russo?" Tevia asks. "The police will want a reason. You can't go blamin' someone with no reason. Besides, she is Koslov's daughter. How are you gonna make him point a finger at his own daughter? You're nuts! He'll never go along with it."

"I wouldn't have to be trying to think of something if you had done your job!" Hugo jumps up and paces again. "Damn fool! You left the tent peg, and that stupid dummy... I told you to tie weights on the body and sink him in the middle of the lake! How much simpler could I make it?"

"I did weigh the body down!" says Tevia, in his own defense. "You'd think he'd be hard to find in nine acres of water. I don't know what happened. He just popped back up, and some damn dog found that tent peg. Then he practically dropped it at Gillespie's feet. What was I supposed to do?"

"Well, we're stuck here now. We'll have to wait," Hugo says. "I'll talk to Koslov tomorrow. Maybe he can help us figure out what to do, but we have to stop him from talking to Dania. She doesn't know anything yet. We have to keep her in the dark."

Hugo and Dania pull into the parking lot at Newton-Wellesley Hospital Wednesday morning just after ten. They walk to the elevator, but do not speak as they ride to the second floor where Boris Koslov's room is located. They approach the nurse's station.

"Mr. Koslov is waiting for the release form from his doctor, and then he may leave. You are here to take him home?" The nurse smiles at Dania. "You could go down and pay the bill while he's waiting for the doctor. He will be along shortly."

Hugo and Dania go to Boris's room. He is dressed and impatiently waiting in a chair.

"Well, it's about time," Koslov complains. "*Chuccuo*, I've been waiting all morning to leave this place. I hate hospitals! They smell and give me boils!"

"We have to wait for the doctor to discharge you," Dania says. "I'll go down, take care of the bill, and be right back. We'll have you home soon." Dania kisses her father's cheek, pats his shoulder, and quickly leaves the room.

"How much does she know?" Koslov asks.

"Nothing," replies Hugo. "She's been asking questions, but she doesn't suspect anything." Hugo sits on the edge of the bed facing Koslov. "I blame Tevia. He screwed up, and now there's all kind of trouble."

"It could have waited 'til I was out of this wretched place!" He lowers his voice. "I didn't want him killed. I wanted my money back! I told ju I would handle it. He would have given my money back, and then maybe I'd have killed him."

"What if he'd already spent the money? What would you have done then?" asks Hugo.

"Don't be stupid. He took it on Friday and died Saturday night. What? He bought another carnival with it?" Koslov makes a Russian sound deep in his throat to demonstrate his disgust. "At least I would have it back. Now what do we do?" asks Koslov—getting even more irritated. "Maybe we wait until the police find it, huh? How is that going to help me?"

"Look, I did what I thought you wanted."

"*Cuya moi*, ju thought wrong!"

Dania and the doctor enter the room. "See, it took only a few minutes and a couple questions for the doctor to sign your release. Now we can go home."

95

"Here is a prescription for dizziness and headaches. Take it as noted, and don't take more than six a day. If the symptoms persist longer than a week, call me." Dr. Skornick hands it to Dania and leaves.

Koslov makes a rude gesture the doctor does not see. The nurse pushes a wheelchair into the room. She helps him into the chair, wheels him down in the elevator, and out the door. Koslov does not say another word until they are safely in the car. ""*Cuya moi!*" he says as they pull away.

The ride back to the carnival is made in stony silence. The only sound is the *thrup-thrup* of the car's windshield wipers. Dania tries to engage her father with small talk, but he is mute. Hugo is the same. She knows something has transpired between these two men. She will get to the bottom of it, one way or another. She will wait 'til she has her father alone.

The police are wasting no time in talking to Koslov. They are waiting by Koslov's trailer dressed in rain slickers with their hats pulled down against the rain. They watch the big black car splash through the mud in its approach.

Gillespie opens the back door of the car when it comes to a stop. "I wish I could give you more time to recuperate, but I know you are anxious to be on your way. I am sorry. I'll be as brief as possible, but we need to talk."

Hugo helps Koslov into the trailer and into his chair at the desk. The police stay outside, but Dania and Gillespie enter.

"Do any of you recognize this handkerchief?" Gillespie asks when they are all seated. The room is close and damp. Gillespie hands it to Koslov, who looks at it and shakes his head. He hands it to Dania, but she doesn't recognize it either, and hands it to Hugo.

"Yes, I do!" Hugo exclaims, jumping up from his seat.

Tony may come over and sit on the porch with her every evening after supper, but only for an hour—Donal's rule. Ellen has also agreed that if her grades slip, this privilege will end.

"Part of growing up is not forgetting your responsibilities," Ellen often reminds Christopher whenever he forgets some task like taking out the trash. He usually has some funny remark to make, but she takes it seriously.

For now, her responsibilities are chores and homework, but soon these will change as she graduates high school and starts in college. Ellen has always been a straight A student, and Moira and Donal would like to see all their children go to college. Michael chose to work in the mill after graduation from Our Lady's, in order to help the family financially. Then the accident occurred, and everyone felt he'd made the right decision.

Donal listens to their conversations on the porch. He doesn't think it's eavesdropping. He's protecting his daughter's reputation, and it was Moira's requirement if Tony was to visit. Ellen had mentioned that soon it would be too cold to sit on the porch. Would they allow Tony to visit her inside? Neither one had answered. Donal is so proud of Ellen right now. He thinks she has a damn good head on her shoulders; she takes after her mother. If he could get Michael to settle down and marry a nice Irish girl, he just might have a chance for grandchildren to boast about.

The two love birds are sitting on the front porch. "Ellen," Tony says, breaking the contented silence. "What will you do after graduation? I know your father would like you to go to college. Is that what you want?"

"I've been thinking about that," Ellen says. ""There are several nearby colleges. I have sent letters to a couple to see what they offer. I thought about being a nurse or a secretary, but I like children, and teaching school is something I think I want to do."

"What about us, Ellen?" Tony asks, taking her hand in his. ""Maybe after graduation we could get engaged . . . or something." Tony blushes under his dark complexion. "I have never cared for anyone the way I feel for you. Ellen, I love you."

"Oh, Tony, I feel the same, but we need time to be sure." She turns in her chair and looks directly into his eyes. "Loving someone is special. I'm only seventeen. I want you. I want college. Imagine how good our life would be once I get a degree. I'd have everything I want."

"I know you're right," he says. "This is so hard for me. I'm older, but you're more grown up. I put in for a promotion at the mill. I'm going to settle down and try real hard to be someone you can be proud of. I want to take care of you properly. Ellen, can we think about getting engaged after graduation?"

"I don't know. You know you'll have to ask my father for my hand."

"Aw, shit, I forgot about that!"

Ellen can't help herself and laughs.

Donal takes out his pocket watch. Checking the time, he calls out the window. "Tony, it's time for you to hit the road."

"He's going, Da," Ellen calls back.

Tony suddenly takes Ellen by the shoulders and kisses her gently on the mouth. Stepping back, he gives her a nod and a wink. "First time I ever kissed a teacher," he jokes. In that moment they both know that things are going to be just fine.

Donal is peeking from behind the front room curtains.

"Moira is going to kill me," he whispers.

Lieutenant Gillespie stands on the door step of Mrs. Russo's small, run-down house on Dalby Street. The paint on the siding is worn through, exposing wooden shingles. Gillespie feels that any minute the porch could give way.

"Mrs. Russo, I know this is unpleasant, but it's necessary if we're to figure out why your son was killed," Lieutenant Gillespie says calmly and politely. "We'd like to take a look around the house to see if we can find anything that might help."

"I don't understand any of this," she says through the screen door. "He was a good boy. Maybe he was a little headstrong. Sometimes he rubbed people the wrong way, but my Johnny didn't deserve to be thrown in Silver Lake like he was." She is crying.

"We are just trying to help, Mrs. Russo. Maybe his father could be of some help? May we come in and talk while my men have a look around?" Gillespie opens the screen door, guides Mrs. Russo into the living room, and helps her to the couch. He takes a chair opposite her, and pulls out his notebook. He nods to his men to start looking around.

"Johnny's father left before Johnny was born," Rose Russo answers. "The boy never even met him. James Russo was his name. He went to war and never came back. I didn't know I was pregnant until after he shipped out. I sent him a letter, but he never answered. Then I heard he was killed in action. It was just me and Johnny, and I did the best I could."

The lieutenant observes the woman. Her harsh life is etched on her face. Her salt and pepper hair is pulled tight back in a low bun, and loose strands dangle down her neck. Her clothes are thin from repeated washing and hang on her thin frame. Her eyes are red rimmed and filled with unshed tears.

"Did Johnny have any enemies that you know of? Anyone he mentioned that might have had it in for him?"

"The only thing I can think of is the other night when he got let go at the Carnival. He worked the booths for every carnival that came to town. We needed money," Rose says. "He came home all upset because they replaced him and told him not to come back."

"Did he say why he was let go?" asks the lieutenant.

"No, he didn't, but he was pretty mad about it. He went back to try and get his job back, but that big guy, Hugo, told him to get lost."

"Did Johnny say why they fired him?" asks Gillespie again.

"No, he never said why." Rose reaches for the handkerchief inside the top of her dress and wipes her eyes. "I told him something else would come along. He was going to ask the taverns and breweries along Bottle Alley for work. They sometimes have jobs sweeping up or loading the drays. Johnny didn't take to schooling. He wasn't much good with reading or numbers. He worked at the mills for a while but couldn't get on for a permanent job."

Gillespie makes a note to ask Hugo why he had fired Russo. The connection to the carnival had just gotten stronger.

"Lieutenant, could you look at this?" One of the men calls from the doorway.

"Excuse me, Mrs. Russo. I'll be right back," He gets up and follows the officer to Johnny's bedroom. Officer Drew shows him a black leather bag with a couple hundred dollars cash inside.

"We found this stuffed in here," Drew says, pointing at the closet.

"Things are starting to come together. This must be the missing money," says Gillespie.

Lieutenant Gillespie and Officer Drew take the bag back to Mrs. Russo. "Mrs. Russo, have you seen this before?" the lieutenant asks.

"No. No, I don't believe so. Why?"

"We found it in the back of Johnny's closet. We believe it's the stolen money from the carnival. There's a couple hundred dollars here."

"My Johnny would never do something like that. He's— he was a good boy!" Mrs. Russo cries breaking down.

100

"Did he have any extra money around when he died?" Gillespie keeps prodding. "I know this is hard, but it's important."

Rose takes a deep breath, and sighs. "He gave me money for the rent. We were a bit behind, and he gave me enough to catch up. He said he saved up for it, and I believed him."

"Mrs. Russo, I'm very sorry for your loss. We'll be going and leave you in peace. Do you have any questions for me?" Lieutenant Gillespie offers as he stands and puts his hat on.

"No, but thank you," Rose says as she gets up from the battered couch. She walks them to the door. "Father Gallagher has been around a couple times and is helping me with the arrangements."

Lieutenant Gillespie follows his men out the door, tipping his hat to Mrs. Russo as he says good-bye. "Let's go ask Hugo and Koslov a couple of questions." I have a funny feeling about all this."

After supper the next day, Michael takes a walk down to Hawthorn Street, avoiding puddles. It is raining again. Dania has been on his mind all day, and he hopes to meet up with her. There is a lot of activity going on. Trailers are being packed, and some are moving out. He is relieved when he spots Dania talking heatedly to Hugo, and he heads in that direction.

"Be thankful he is letting the carnival move on at all," says Dania. She is sorting through a large box. Michael assumes it must be her fortune-telling equipment. He can make out colorful fabrics spilling over the side as she digs through the contents.

"I should be allowed to go with the carnival. I'm next in charge after your father," Hugo rants.

Michael keeps his distance until he sees Hugo storm off. "Are you leaving?" he asks walking up to her.

"I'm not; the carnival is finally moving on," she informs him. "Lieutenant Gillespie is letting everyone go, but Hugo, Tevia, my father, and I have to stay a while longer. He still believes Johnny Russo's death and the robbery have something to do with the carnival."

Michael is pleased she is staying on one hand, but he has mixed feelings... *if I'm falling in love with her, it will break my heart when she leaves.*

"Michael, I have to ask you something,"Dania says. "Did you have anything to do with Johnny Russo's murder...even if it was an accident... and you panicked?"

"How can you think that? I would never do anything like that. I didn't even know him." Michael is shocked and angered by the question.

"Lieutenant Gillespie showed us the kerchief that was used to tie Russo's hands. Hugo said it was yours. I couldn't believe it, but I saw you wearing one just like it. I was starting to like you, now this. You are also a suspect. How could I be so stupid . . . to like a gorja." She turns to walk away.

"Dania, wait. I didn't have anything to do with the robbery or Johnny's death." She keeps walking. Michael calls after her. "I hardly knew him. I lost my kerchief that first night I worked. I came back the next day and looked for it, but couldn't find it." He runs after her, catches her, and turns her to face him. "I'm telling you the truth."

There are tears in her eyes, and she shakes her head slowly. The rain is falling steadily now, and they are both soaked through to the skin. Michael places his hands on either side of her face. He uses his thumbs to wipe the rain and tears from her cheeks, but it is a losing battle.

"Please, let's talk about this. Can we go to your trailer and get out of this rain?"

They walk quickly, heads down, dodging puddles. Michael jumps ahead and opens the door to let her go first. The trailer is warm and cozy. He takes off his wet jacket and cap. Dania shakes out her wet shawl and places the garments over a rack to dry. She grabs a couple of towels to dry their hair. The rest of their clothes are wet as well but will have to wait.

Dania busies herself putting a pot of coffee on the stove and getting some cups from the small cupboard above the sink. She sits opposite Michael at the table and brushes tendrils of wet hair from her face. Michael has never seen a woman as perfect and as beautiful as Dania is at that moment. *She takes my breath away. I can't speak; Hell, I can't even think straight.* "Now what do we do?" Michael asks.

"I don't know," Dania says. "I don't believe you robbed my father, and I don't believe that you killed Johnny, but it's not looking good with Hugo pointing the police in your direction. What reason would he have to do that?" The coffee is ready. Dania fills both cups with the steaming liquid, and places milk and sugar on the table.

"There is only one reason I can think of," says Michael, stirring sugar and milk into his cup. "He's trying to throw suspicion away from himself. I don't think he robbed your father, but I do think he had something to do with Russo's murder."

"Why would you think that? He's my cousin—my father's right hand."

"It's just a feeling I have. I believe he's protecting himself, that's all," says Michael.

A strained silence follows. Dania looks at Michael with his sandy hair awry and his blue eyes so appealing. She scrunches her hair with the towel, knowing it will take some time to dry.

Michael watches her, knowing that he will hate every minute they aren't together from this moment on. How will life be when she leaves? How will he be able to go on? They sip, quietly observing the other, until the cups are empty.

"Maybe I should go so you can get into dry clothes. Can we talk tomorrow evening? Why don't I take you over to Sullivan's for a meal? It's a Friday night; no work for either of us on Saturday. I'll even bring an umbrella, just in case it's still raining. What do you say?"

"Okay, about eight o'clock?" She stands up and clears the table. Michael picks up his coat and cap, still damp and cold from the rain. He walks to the door and down the couple of steps from the trailer. He avoids a growing puddle at the bottom, turns, and looks up at Dania. She is framed by the opening, and the light behind her makes her red hair glow like fire. *God, I have never wanted anyone so much as I want her.*

He walks home, head down against the rain, and does not notice he is being watched. Hugo watches from the shadows. He doesn't like that mick hanging around Dania. She is his property! It suddenly dawns on him that he's jealous. He's confused. She's his cousin . . . Could he possibly want her in that way? No, but he wants the control, the power. He wants to be in charge, of her *and* the carnival. Boris Koslov is in his way. To have the carnival and keep the secret about Russo's murder, Koslov would have to go, but how? Hugo is confident, he'll find a way. Maybe the mick could get blamed for Koslov's death, too. How wonderful; two for one. He saunters back to his trailer to plot the murder of Boris Koslov.

Tevia sits in Hugo's cramped trailer; sipping hot coffee and listening to Hugo go on about how to get rid of Koslov.

104

Hugo paces the same five feet, back and forth; the only clear space in the mess he calls home.

"The blame has to fall on that Irish Mick," Hugo says. "I need him out of the way. Dania is falling for him, I can tell. She must travel with the carnival; I won't allow her to stay behind with him. We have to think of something!"

"What's this *we*?" Tevia asks. "Killing Russo was a mistake. Boris just wanted him roughed up so he'd give back the money he stole. He can't tell us where the money is, and now you want Boris killed so he can't talk about what happened? Are you out of your mind?"

CHAPTER FOURTEEN

It is eight o'clock sharp on another rainy night when Michael knocks at Dania's door. She quickly answers.

"Hello, I see you're ready," Michael says. "I brought an umbrella this time."

"That was thoughtful. She links her arm with his, and they begin walking.

"Michael, the police were here again. They found my father's money—what was left of it—at Johnny Russo's house. He's the one who robbed us. They're convinced that someone from the carnival found out he did it and killed him for it."

"Okay, but why not get the money back first?" he asks.

"Maybe, whoever did it wasn't after the money but had another reason to kill him and it's just a coincidence. They're asking about Johnny getting fired," she pauses, "and you taking his place. Did you know that?"

"I saw Johnny leave that night after talking to Koslov. He was mad. He said he was let go. I thought Koslov would give him another booth."

"Let's not talk about this now." Dania takes his hand and picks up the pace. "I'm starved."

They are waiting to cross Watertown Street when Michael sees Tony and Ellen coming. They are huddled under an umbrella as they stroll down Bottle Alley in their direction. Tony waves, and Ellen wears a big smile. Dania and Michael meet them in front of Sullivan's Tavern, where the air is filled with the aroma of shepherd's pie and spaghetti and meatballs.

"What are you doing here?" Michael asks.

"Would you believe that Ma and Da said that we can take a walk together tonight," Ellen says excitedly.

"Yeah, I even had the nerve to ask if I could take Ellen to the pictures, and they said maybe." Tony kisses her hand, and then adds, "But it will all depend on what's playing."

"Well, that's a switch," Michael says. "This is my friend Dania. Dania, my sister Ellen, and I think you know Tony. We're going in for dinner."

"It's nice to meet you, Dania. I hope we'll see you again," Ellen gazes fondly up at Tony. "Come on, Tony, we better be going." Ellen loops her arm in Tony's and pulls him along.

"Those two have it bad," Dania says, watching the couple walk away. "They are heading toward the park on the corner of Bridge and Watertown Streets. I have an idea they'll be warming a bench for a bit."

"That's my baby sister and best friend you're talking about." He laughs as he closes the umbrella, takes her hand, and leads her up the steps and into the restaurant.

The night is chilly. Hugo and Tevia have been drinking for over an hour in Hugo's trailer. The bottle of vodka sits between them, almost empty. The ashtray is overflowing with cigarette butts. Hugo looks at the propane heater. He opens the front casing, checks inside, and taking a match lights it up.

"I can tell you're up to something," Tevia says.

"You don't want to know," replies Hugo.

"Well, I'm going to bed." Tevia stands and stretches. He grabs his coat and opens the door. "Don't do anything stupid." He throws his coat over his head and steps out into the rain.

Hugo waits a few minutes, pacing the small space, thinking. He makes up his mind, grabs another bottle of vodka under the sink, and rushes out the door and over to Koslov's trailer. He goes in without knocking.

"Tevia's gone to bed, and I have this whole bottle of vodka to share," Hugo says companionably. He takes a couple glasses from a cupboard, places one in front of Koslov, and puts one for himself on the table.

"Why are ju so happy?" Koslov asks, watching Hugo pour the clear liquid.

"Soon all our problems will disappear and we can be on our way to the sunshine for the winter."

"How do ju figure that, my friend?" Koslov asks, taking a long, slow drink. Hugo wastes no time in refilling the glass.

"That Irish friend of Dania's, he is going to be blamed for murder. Then we can go."

"How do ju know that? Has Gillespie been here?" Koslov asks. He does not notice that his glass is refilled each time he takes a drink.

"Gillespie is just a stupid *Mick* with a badge. I'll show him who did it, and he will believe it." Hugo speaks with such confidence, it worries Koslov.

"I think ju underestimate him," Koslov takes another drink. "I also think I'm getting old. I can't drink like I used to."

Hugo reaches over and strikes a match, turning on Koslov's heater. He turns it on high.

"It's not cold enough for the heater yet. I like it cold to sleep. It reminds me of home in Russia. I dream of home sometimes." Koslov gets up and stumbles to his bed. "Maybe I will go back some day. For now, I will dream." He falls into bed, and in minutes he is in a deep vodka-fueled sleep, snoring loudly.

Hugo smashes the half empty vodka bottle against the heater. Koslov stirs a little at the sound but doesn't wake. The spilled vodka runs under the heater. Hugo takes a blanket from the bed and throws it over the heater. A corner of the blanket soaks up vodka.

Hugo leaves quickly. He will miss Koslov but feels he has no choice.

The rain is steady, and the noise on the roof keeps Tevia awake. Tevia looks out his window and sees Hugo come out of Koslov's and dash to his own trailer.

Dania and Michael talk about family; his here, and hers in Russia. He learns about life in a carnival and appreciates all that it means to Dania. The carnival is her life and not being with it, or with her father, scares her.

He is happy with his life in Newton. He tells her about Tony and the trouble they got into as kids. How they skated on Silver Lake in the winter and took the bus to Normbega Park in the summer. She is fascinated by the park where they can picnic, canoe, ride the carousel, and visit the zoo. He says he'd like to take her to the Totem Pole Ballroom before she leaves. Maybe one of the big bands will be playing.

They talk until closing time. Sullivan follows them to the door and locks it behind them. Michael opens the umbrella, and they huddle together as they cross the street and walk up Bottle Alley to where the travel trailers are parked. Inside the gates they jump around the growing puddles of rain water to reach Dania's trailer. She hesitates on the steps.

"I had a wonderful time, Michael." She doesn't want to go inside yet. "Thank you." She knows inviting Michael in at this hour is not a good idea, considering the way she feels about him.

"Me, too."

"I would ask you to come in. . ."

"We probably shouldn't."

She sees her father's trailer. "Oh, my God, I think it's on fire!" She jumps off the step and runs. "Papa! Papa! Help! Fire!"

Michael is behind her and stops her from running into the burning trailer.

"Not so fast! Be careful." He feels the doorknob. "It's warm, but not hot."

"Go get help," he tells her. "Get Tevia or Hugo to pull the fire alarm on the corner. Go now. I'll get your father."

Michael carefully opens the door. The fresh air feeds the fire, and in seconds it spreads. At first all he can make out are fire and smoke. Then he cautiously steps in. He sees Koslov on the bed, unconscious. The fire has reached the bed where the man lies.

"Koslov, Koslov . . . you better not be dead!" Michael coughs, smoke filling his lungs. "Koslov, get up before we both burn."

The old man rouses. Michael pulls him to his feet. They stagger to the door and down the steps, collapsing on the wet ground. There is a sudden whoosh, and the fire surges through the doorway. Windows explode, and the trailer is engulfed with smoke and flames dancing on the roof.

Michael gets Koslov to his feet and helps him over to sit on Dania's steps. They hear the fire bells in the distance. Dania rushes up and hugs her father. He is shivering in his rain-soaked clothes.

"Help me get him inside." Michael and Dania guide her father up the steps and into the trailer. They put him down on one of the beds. She gets towels to dry him off and covers him with a blanket. Michael heats up some coffee for them. More sirens sound in the distance.

"You have any whisky for the coffee?" asks Michael.

""Under the sink," she replies.

An explosion rents the air as the propane tank on Koslov's trailer explodes.

"What's happening?" Koslov exclaims, startled by the sudden noise.

"You're safe now, Papa."Dania gently pushes him back down on the bed.

The lights from the arriving fire trucks reflect through the windows. Shouts and commands are heard along with the sound of approaching police sirens.

"My guess is that's Lieutenant Gillespie coming to join the party," says Michael, looking out the door. Tevia rushes up, breathless from running.

"Is Boris okay?" asks Tevia. "It looks like his trailer is a goner."

"Where's Hugo?"Dania asks. "I'm surprised he's not here."

"I saw him earlier leaving your father's place. I haven't seen him since."

"I wonder where he went. You would think all the noise would bring him running," Dania says, scanning the gathering crowd of onlookers.

Lieutenant Gillespie pulls up in front. He gets out of the squad car and slams the door, hard. His driver winces. The expression on Gillespie's haggard face tells them he is not happy to be back.

"Can't these people stay out of my hair for a while?" Gillespie grumbles to himself. "I haven't solved the break in, the assault on Koslov, or who killed Johnny Russo, and now this!"

"Lieutenant, I'm sure this is just an unfortunate accident," Michael says, his arms around Dania, comforting her.

"We'll see what the arson team has to say," the lieutenant counters. "Anyone hurt?"

"My father is in here," says Dania. "He would have burned to death, but Michael went in and got him out just before it blew up. Papa is resting. It's a lot for an old man to go through."

"Let's see what he can tell us—if he remembers anything." He climbs the steps and gives a brief knock before walking into the bedroom. "Police. I'm coming in, Koslov."

Boris is on the bed bundled up in a blanket, but awake and waiting for the lieutenant. Gillespie pulls over a chair and sits beside the bed.

"Well, well. Here we are again, Boris," Gillespie pulls out his notebook. "Can you tell me about tonight and how the fire might have started?" The lieutenant is almost kind to the old man. He can tell that the fire and almost burning to death has him shaken up.

"Hugo and I were sitting around talking and drinking," says Boris. He closes his eyes; his brow furrows as he tries to remember. His mind is still in a vodka fog. "We were just old friends passing the time. The vodka was getting to me, so I went to lie down. I must have passed out because the next thing I know, the boy is shouting at me to get up if I want to live. He drags me over here, and now ju are here again. That's all I know."

"You're a very lucky man, Boris." Gillespie puts the notebook and pen in his pocket. "We are going to take a look and see if we can figure out how the fire started. I'll leave you to rest and go talk to the others." He puts the chair back where he got it from and leaves.

Gillespie steps out of the trailer. "Michael, I want to know what you saw from the time you arrived until you rescued Koslov."

"I don't have much to tell," says Michael. "Dania and I had gone out to dinner. It was raining pretty hard on the way back, and we were rushing. She noticed the fire. I told her to find Hugo or Tevia and have someone ring the alarm. Koslov was on the bed, and the fire was all around. I grabbed him and got him out the door just as the whole trailer exploded."

Michael shakes his hand. "Thank you, Lieutenant, for coming so quickly."

"We appreciate you looking into it."Dania says, as Gillespie leaves. The lieutenant gets into the squad car—closing the door softer this time. The car splashes its way back to Watertown Street.

As the squad car passes through the gates, Hugo strolls up from the opposite direction.

"Where have you been?" Dania is furious. "Papa almost died. His trailer caught fire."

"What do you mean almost died?" Hugo can barely hide how stunned he is that Boris is still alive.

"Michael saved him! He risked his life to bring Papa out of the fire!"

Hugo sits down on the steps, shaking his head, unable to believe what he's hearing. ""The damn Irish chucco messed up my perfect plan," he mutters to himself.

"I'd better get going, Dania. The family will be wondering where I am. I'll stop by tomorrow and see how you're doing."

Michael leans over and gives Dania a delicate kiss on the lips. He wants to hold and comfort her. He wants to protect her from all the evil in the world. He realizes at this moment that this must be what it feels like to love someone. Damn it all to hell! He's in love with Dania, a carnival fortuneteller. He can already hear his mother; if the heart attack she'll have doesn't kill her first.

"Hi, Ma." Michael walks into the warm kitchen. He takes off his wet things and hangs them in the back hall to dry out.

"Where have you been? You smell of smoke. I heard the engines leaving the station, and they didn't go far."

""One of the carnival trailers caught on fire." He tries to sound casual. "It's late. How is it you're still up?" Michael asks.

"Oh, I'm nosy," Moira says. "I was sitting with your Da when we heard the sirens. We could smell the smoke from here. Was anyone hurt?"

Here it is—the dreaded inquisition. If he doesn't tell her everything, she will find out eventually. She always does.

"Is Da still up? I can tell you both together—much easier than telling it twice."

"Why don't you go see, and I'll be along in a minute."

Michael walks quietly down the hall in case his father is asleep already. Donal is sitting in his chair by the window. He has the lights off, which Michael thinks is strange.

""Da, you okay?"

"Oh, I'm fine. I was watching the glow from the fire for a while. It's too cold to sit outside tonight, and all the rain makes it damp." Donal turns to Michael. "Did you go have a look?"

"I kind of had a front row seat."

Moira comes into the room and sits in the old platform rocker. Michael sits on the piano bench. He takes a deep breath and begins.

"I went to Sullivan's for a meal with a friend," Michael begins, wondering how to bring up the subject of Dania. "On our way out, we saw that one of the carnival trailers was on fire. There was a man inside, unconscious. I helped him get out, waited for the fire department, and the police. I had to give a statement."

"Well, I suppose that friend was a gypsy named Dania," Moira says. Donal and Michael exchange surprised looks.

"How in heaven's name do you know these things?" Michael asks. "You don't even have to leave the house!"

"I've been trying to figure that out since the day I met your mother," Donal says.

"What I want to know is why in the name of St. Patrick and all the saints, you have to get mixed up with a gypsy... from a carnival of all things. There are plenty of nice Irish Catholic girls around," Moira is heated. "You know what I think of carnivals and the people that run them. I had to find out from Mrs. O'Leary, who lives on Adams Street across from the church. From what she tells me, you and this Dania are pretty close. The only reason that girl is still here is because of all the trouble and that poor Johnny Russo."

"Ma, I like her a lot. More than any girl I've ever met. Ma, I might even love her." Michael holds his breath and waits for the storm he knows will follow. This is the first time he's ever told anyone about his feelings for Dania. He's not even told her yet.

"Well, I guess you had better bring her around," Donal says. "Bring her for Sunday lunch, about 2 pm. That okay with you, Moira?"

"I suppose we'd better meet her. Let's see what kind of a girl has stolen my Michael's heart."

116

CHAPTER FIFTEEN

Dania sits beside her father and watches him snore in the night. Dr. Skornick had wanted him to go to the hospital, but the stubborn old Russian was not going back to Newton-Wesley Hospital unless he was dead. Even though Dania had battled her father, Boris was determined not to go. Dr. Skornick had given up, left some pills to help clear his chest, and said he'd be back.

It's almost daylight on Saturday morning when Dania finally drifts off for a couple hours. She wakes to hammering on her door. She stumbles to the door, half asleep.

"Lieutenant Gillespie, back so soon?"Dania sighs, resigned to having the police in her life forever it seems. ""Come on in. I'll put the coffee on."

Boris stirs. "What's all the noise? Can't a man die in peace?" Boris moans, holding his head from the hangover. "Dania, get me some aspirin. My head is exploding."

He sits up and sees Gillespie sitting at the small table. "Ju back again?" He swings his legs over the side of the bed and sits up. "Oh, my God, what did I do last night? I don't remember a thing. Dania, why am I in ju'r place and not mine? Where is that aspirin... and get me coffee, too!"

Dania places the aspirin bottle in her father's hands along with a glass of water. She puts a cup of coffee on the table near his bed. Boris fumbles with the aspirin bottle. He manages to get a couple pills out and chokes them down with the water. He drinks it all and hands the empty glass and aspirin bottle back to her. "I feel better knowing relief is coming. So Gillespie, what brings ju back to see us this time? Can't leave us alone?"

"How much of last night do you remember, Koslov?" asks the lieutenant.

"Let's see. I was playing cards with Hugo and Tevia in the afternoon. We were sharing a bottle of vodka. The vodka hit me hard. Never since I was a young fool in Russia did it hit me so quick. I went back to my trailer, and that's all I remember. Did something happen to Hugo or Tevia? Tell me! What's going on?" He coughs.

"Last night a fire destroyed your trailer. You barely made it out alive. Dania's friend Michael got you out just before the gas heater blew up," Gillespie says. Boris can only stare at him in disbelief.

"How did it catch fire?" Boris asks, afraid of the answer.

"We think the propane heater was on. A blanket and a smashed vodka bottle were found. It was a recipe for fire."

"I could not have turned on the heater. At least I don't think I did." Boris massages his sore head. "No, I didn't turn it on. I was passed out. Ju can ask Hugo."

Koslov's mind is going over as much as he can remember of the previous night. Hugo was in his trailer... going to bed... Suddenly, the splintering crash of the vodka bottle bursts through the haze. Hugo had broken the bottle and set everything up to look like an accident. What an old fool he was to have trusted Hugo. He'll take care of him and maybe Tevia too. He coughs.

"We need to question Hugo and Tevia and see if they saw anything," the lieutenant says.

"Dania, I know we got your statement last night, but have you remembered anything since we talked?"

118

"There is something Hugo said . . . ," Dania hesitates, thinking. "When I went for help, I stopped at Hugo's trailer first. It's the closest. He wasn't there, so I went and got Tevia. Tevia rang the fire alarm. Afterwards, I saw Hugo coming from behind the trailers. I asked him where he'd been, and he said he was at Sullivan's all evening. He lied. Michael and I were at Sullivan's and didn't see him there. Jack Sullivan locked up as we left. Why would Hugo lie about where he was? He couldn't have been coming from Sullivan's."

"Hugo's been with me for years, ever since Russia. His mother was my sister. His father died before he was born, and my sister ran away from the circus. Later, I heard she had died and went to find her son. He was in an orphanage, but I wanted him to have a better life. Hugo has been like a son to me. He is going to take over the business from me someday." Boris tries to stand then slumps back down on the bed, coughing badly. Dania rushes for the medicine the doctor left. The coughing worries her.

Lieutenant Gillespie stands, his head almost touching the low ceiling. "I'll see what Tevia and Hugo have to say and leave you two to rest."

She walks him to the door.

"Dania, if you remember anything else, or just want to talk, you have my number."

Michael is on his second cup of coffee sitting at the breakfast table with the whole family telling what happened.

"I can't get over it. You're a hero!" Christopher exclaims. His brother Michael is now ten feet tall in his eyes.

"Did you get grilled by the cops?" Frank asks. He is obsessed with the current gangster movies. George Raft is a favorite of his, much to his mother's dismay.

119

"I'm not a hero, and I didn't get *grilled* by the cops. I just did what needed to be done and then gave a statement to the police."

"Ma says you're inviting your friend Dania to Sunday lunch," Ellen says, helping to clear the dishes from the table. Ellen leans over and whispers in Michael's ear. "Ma said I can ask Tony, too."

"Quit dawdling, you lot. Michael, take your brothers and make a pen for the chickens between the two sheds down back. That pen they're in now has flooded, and the chickens will have to learn to swim if they stay there. Ellen, you can help in the garden during this break from the rain. We need to pick some of the vegetables while we can."

"I heard the weather report on the radio last night," Donal says. "There's a storm off the coast moving this way. They're saying it's a hurricane and pushing all the rain in front of it. We're in for some high winds and more rain before it's over. They can't say where it's going yet."

One by one they go about the day's chores. Ellen pulls on her boots and jacket and goes to pick vegetables. Michael gives Christopher and Frank a list of supplies to gather for the new pen. Moira finishes the breakfast dishes and pours Donal another cup of coffee. He is feeling much better these last few days and is spending more time in the kitchen with her and the children. Moira is glad of his company again. She no longer worries so much about him, and the children have their Da back.

Moira is drying her hands on a towel. ""I think we'll use the dining room tomorrow for lunch. We'll need the extra room. We'll set it up after church."

"You're up to something, old girl, inviting a Russian fortuneteller and a young Italian boy to Sunday lunch." Donal taps his chin. "Are you going to *grill* them? Try to see what their intentions are?" he laughs.

"Yes, in a way," she admits. "This Dania; we know nothing about her. Michael fancies her, and I'm worried. She's not what I wanted for him. She's Russian. Is she Catholic? She's part of a carnival. What kind of life has she had? The police are involved. I want to know what and who he's getting mixed up with. For all we know she might have killed Johnny Russo."

"Now you're just borrowing trouble. I don't believe for a second that Michael would be involved with her if he thought she was capable of something like that."

"I'm not so sure."

"You did a good job raising him. Now just sit back and see how well it took."

Moira looks out the window at the overcast sky. "You say there's a storm heading our way?"

"You know they can never tell about a hurricane. They usually veer off at the last minute, and we've all worried for nothing."

"At least the chickens won't drown in their new pen. Although, if it keeps raining like it has, we won't be able to put them in the new pen anyway. What's left in the vegetable garden is ruined as well. The potatoes are going bad, along with the lettuce. Even the winter squash has to be pulled up early."

"We'll save what we can," he says.

"I'll have Christopher and Frank help in the garden this afternoon. Do you think you might be able to watch over them while they do it? If it's not raining cats and dogs, that is."

"Sure I can." He pats her hand. "I can get up and down the path. I only need to tell them what to pick. They can do all the bending and lifting." Donal is happy to be useful again.

121

After supper Tony calls around for Ellen. Moira and Donal are getting used to the idea of Ellen dating an Italian. Tony asks if he can take Ellen out for ice cream, and they agree. The couple hurries off. Christopher and Frank get into a wild game of dominos with Donal. Moira rocks away in her chair and listens to their laughter as she works on an afghan. She smiles softly wishing every night could be this peaceful.

"I've been talking to my folks about you," Tony confesses. "They know I've been going over to your house, but I never told them about how I want to marry you some day. Mom knew even before I did that I love you, she says. How do mothers do that, I wonder? She's a lot like your mother. I think you'll like her, and she'll like you if you get to know each other."

"This is hard on both sets of parents. They think they know what's best for us. Michael says things will work out. I have to believe him." Ellen hooks her arm in Tony's and rests her head on his shoulder for a minute.

When they get to the ice cream parlor, all the booths are full. They take two seats at the counter, and their private moment is lost.

Michael heads down Bottle Alley to see Dania. He splashes through puddles along Adams Street toward the fairgrounds beside Our Lady's church and school. He sees that lights are on in Dania's trailer. It's a dismal night, but no rain. Only the thought of seeing her again could drag him out on such a cold and miserable night.

Dania smiles warmly as she greets him at the door. Michael hangs up his coat and hat and sits at the kitchen table.

"Where's your father tonight?" Michael asks, pleased to have time alone with her now that her father has moved in. He would like to kiss her and never stop, but their time alone has

122

always been so brief. He is afraid . . . no, he *knows* his heart will break when she leaves.

"He walked to Sullivan's with Tevia and Hugo," Dania sets coffee on the stove to boil. "I didn't want him out in this night chill because of his cough, but Hugo and Tevia talked him into it."

"Dania, I'm worried about your father. I don't think the fire was an accident, and we both know Hugo was not at Sullivan's like he said."

"Tevia and Hugo have been acting strangely, and they're avoiding me. Even Papa seems to be hiding something."

They sit and talk of many things, mostly about the events of the last few days. They hear shouting. A loud argument outside disturbs their quiet conversation.

"Don't tell me what I can and cannot do," Boris Koslov is heard shouting. "I still own this carnival, and I will do what I think is best. My daughter will not be dragged into this mess!"

Boris stumbles up the trailer steps. As Dania opens the door, he falls in.

"Hello, what a pleasant night . . . tonight," Koslov says, looking up at her from the floor. He wears a drunken grin, but when he sees Michael, his smile quickly fades.

Struggling to get up, Koslov mumbles, "Ju still sniffing around, huh, chuccuo? My daughter is not for the likes of you!"

"That's not fair,"Dania closes the door behind him. "You'd be dead if Michael had not saved your worthless life."

"Ah, cuya moi," Koslov shouts—pushing her out of his way. He staggers past them and falls, face first on his bed, snoring immediately.

"I'd better go. Looks like you may have your hands full tonight."Michael grabs his coat and hat."Dania, my mother has invited you and your father to lunch tomorrow. May I come by around one o'clock to pick you up? Ellen's Tony is coming as well."

"That would be nice. I'm sorry he was so rude. The drink makes him that way."

"Don't worry, I'll see you tomorrow." Michael steps out into the night.

CHAPTER SIXTEEN

Sunday morning brings wind and rain, and the family sits around the table discussing how they might make it to church.

"Christopher, run across the street and see if the Dennisons are taking their car to mass. If they are, ask if you three young ones can go with them. The nuns will be checking who's there and who's not. Lucky nuns, they don't have the long walk in the pouring rain, and the wind is getting worse."

"Ah, Ma, why can't Frank go?"

"Because you're faster and won't spend all day talking to Mrs. Dennison and eating her cookies. Now get a move on."

While Christopher is gone, Moira lays out her plans for Sunday lunch. "Ellen, you will help in the kitchen. Frank will lay out the dining room table. We have a smoked shoulder, carrots, potatoes, cabbage, and turnips to get ready. The shoulder needs to simmer on the stove for a couple of hours before adding the vegetables. I'll put them in after the guests arrive so they don't overcook. Nothing is worse than overcooked vegetables." She pauses to think. "Missed anything? No," she continues. "We can talk a bit and get to know one another before sitting down to the meal." She crosses her fingers in the hope her guests will approve of her menu. She is giving them something typically Irish. She had thought about corned beef and cabbage, but every Irish house serves that. Moira prides herself on her cooking, and she even has a couple of apple pies waiting for desert.

Christopher rushes in the door. "Mrs. Dennison said yes, she will take us. She wants to go early so they can park close."

"Good, let's hope the priest is not long winded today. I need you all back here to help," Moira says.

"Ma, don't worry so. You're the best cook I know, and I know they'll love every bite." Michael puts his arms around her and hugs her close. "Thanks for doing this. It means a lot to me and to Ellen," he says.

"Go on with ya now. Give me some help with these dishes." Moira blinks back a tear and swats at Michael with her dish towel.

The morning goes quickly as Moira prepares the meal, and before she knows it they're back from church.

"We need not have even gone to church this morning," Frank is not happy. "Hardly anyone was there."

"Mrs. Dennison said it was the same upstairs." Going to Sunday mass is not Christopher's idea of fun in any weather. "Guess no one wanted to get wet. Guess we're lucky the Dennisons have a car. Guess the next time we can stay home!"

"Don't you go getting on my nerves, young man!"

"Ma, do you think the Dennisons might let me use their car to pick up Dania and her father? I hate to have them walk in this weather."

"Michael, all you can do is ask. Here, take them a couple of jars of grape jelly. That might help with the asking." She reaches into the pantry and hands him a couple of jars of the rich dark homemade jelly sealed with paraffin wax. "Be sure to thank them for taking the others earlier."

Michael heads for the fairgrounds in the Dennisons' car. The wind is up, and branches sway alarmingly. The entrance between the gates is flooded, and the black Oldsmobile almost stalls. He pulls as close as he can to Dania's trailer. A gust of wind almost takes the car door out of his hand when he opens it. He runs up the steps, knocks, and opens the door without waiting.

Dania is standing in the small kitchen, her hands on her hips—glaring at her father. "The old fool doesn't want to go. Says he's too tired, and doesn't want to go out in the rain. I told him how important this is." She tries once more. "You won't melt. Michael has a car!"

"Listen, Dania. There will be other times, I hope." He turns to Boris. "Mr. Koslov, it's okay if you don't feel up to coming. We can have you come another time." Michael doesn't want to provoke an argument. "Dania, we'd better go. This weather is getting bad."

She gets her coat and wraps a scarf over her head. Michael opens the door, fighting to hold onto it. He helps Dania down the stairs and into the car.

"I hope he'll be okay there by himself." Dania is worried.

"He'll be fine." Michael covers her hand with his. "He'll probably have a good nap. We can bring him back some of Ma's apple pie."

"I'm a little afraid of meeting your family, Michael. In my culture meeting the family is a big deal. It usually means a marriage proposal."

"Oh boy, I didn't mean to mislead you. You know I like you a lot, and I don't want you to leave. I just thought you might like to meet my family, and I want them to meet you. My parents don't trust carnival people, and for Ma to suggest you and your father come to lunch is a big step for her."

When they pull up in front of the house, he runs around the car to open her door. Ellen is waiting with the front door open as they dash up the steps.

"I can't believe it's so nasty out. Da's listening to the radio for the weather report." She helps Dania out of her wet things.

"So glad you could come, Dania. Didn't your father want to come?" Ellen asks.

"No, I'm afraid not. He had a lot of excuses. He's just being hard-headed. It's his loss." Dania is embarrassed. "You and Michael have been very good to me, and I appreciate it." She gives Ellen a sisterly hug.

"Come, meet my father and the rest of the family," Michael takes her hand and guides her to the front room. "Ma will be out in a minute. Da, I would like you to meet my friend, Dania. This is my father, Donal Flannagan."

"Pleased to meet you, Sir," Dania steps forward to shake Donal's hand.

"You didn't tell me she was such a beauty, Michael." Donal says, smiling. "You can call me Donal or Da. Sorry it's so bad out. I've been trying to catch the weather report. It should be on soon."

Moira joins the group—wiping her hands on a dish towel. She greets Dania warmly.

"Hello, I'm Moira, Michael's mother. We're so glad you came. Your father couldn't make it?"

"He's a divia mush. He was out late last night and is not feeling well," Dania says, excusing her father.

"What did you just call him?" asks Moira.

"Sorry, I called him a crazy man," she replies.

Tony pipes up. "I knew what she said." He's rather proud of himself. "It's part of the carnival language. Some of the guys are using it."

"Yes, they are," Dania adds smiling.

Moira slips back into the kitchen to check on the lunch. The others continue talking.

Donal says, "I'm intrigued. It must be exciting—your life with the carnival."

"It's all I know. My parents worked with the circus when I was born, and after my mother died we came to America."

"I have worked on several of the booths. It's a lot of fun." Tony adds, smiling.

"I like the lights, music, and caramel apples, but I think I like cotton candy the best." Ellen takes Tony's hand. "Why don't we go into the dining room?"

As they take their places and get comfortable, Moira calls Ellen and the boys to help bring out the food. Once everything is ready and Moira has taken her seat, all but Dania bow their heads.

"Bless us, Oh Lord, for these our gifts . . ."

Dania looks from one family member to another.

". . . that we are about to receive . . ."

They all have their eyes closed and their hands pressed together. She is touched by the sight.

". . . from Thy bounty, through Christ, Our Lord."

The family and Tony respond, "Amen."

"Thank you. That was very nice, Frank," says Donal.

"Come on, let's eat before it gets cold," Moira suggests.

Dania samples bites of several items. "This is marvelous. My father doesn't know what he's missing."

"You like to try different foods?" Moira asks.

"I love trying out the new dishes everywhere we travel. I began collecting regional cookbooks, but it's no fun cooking for one person."

Michael listens to the chatter around him.

129

"Dania, what carnival words can you teach me?" asks Frank.

"Well, divia means crazy."

"Oh, like Tony?" asks Ellen, and they all laugh.

"Mush, pronounced like the word 'push' means a buddy."

The table talk is pleasant and comfortable, but Michael is occupied with his own thoughts. He is thinking about what Dania said. He looks across the table at her, and it hits him again. *Oh Lord, help me. I* am *in love. Her smile, those deep brown eyes, and the way she laughs with Da. If only she would stay and marry me.* He takes a gulp of water. *Did I just think that? I must be a divia mush, even thinking she would.*

When they're finished, Dania offers to help clear the table. "Thank you, Dania, but we have it. This time you are our guest. Next time we put you to work." Moira motions to the boys to help. "Maybe you can bring a couple of those cook books. I'd like to see them. We could try a couple of them out."

"I'd like that very much," says Dania. Her heart is warming to this large Irish family. The carnival has always been her family, but there is so much more here. There's love that she has never felt before. Could she leave the carnival and stay here? Would Michael want that?

Frank comes rushing up. "It's the weatherman. He says a hurricane is coming. Da what's a hurricane?"

"Let's go listen," Donal says, motioning for a hand up. Michael and Tony help him to his chair. Donal turns the radio up.

The weatherman's voice is tense as he speaks. "We are in for a bad few hours here in Boston. A fierce storm has just ripped through Long Island with winds gusting to one hundred miles an hour. This is a fast-moving storm traveling at sixty miles an hour. We expect major flooding in and around the Boston area. It is unknown at this time where exactly the storm will go, but it will

hit Massachusetts. Everyone is advised to stay indoors." The
listeners could hear the weatherman flipping pages. "This just in:
Long Island has been devastated by the storm, and we expect high
casualties in that area. Again, stay indoors! Trees and large
branches are in danger of falling. Stay away from downed
electrical wires. This has been Larry Gardino with your local
weather. We will keep you updated on the storm's progress." The
report ended and the station returned to music.

"Oh no, Papa is alone in the trailer."

"Michael, you and Tony take Dania and get her father to
come back here," Donal demands.

"Yes, he must come here. A trailer is no place to be in a
storm like this," says Moira.

"You are too kind. I can't ask that of you," says Dania.

"You didn't ask; we are offering. You must both stay here
until it is safe to go back."

Michael already has their coats. Tony takes Ellen's hand
and kisses it. Then to the surprise of all—including himself—he
kisses her boldly on the lips. "But before I go, I want to know one
thing." Getting down on one knee he takes Ellen's hand. "Ellen
Flannigan, will you marry me?"

The family is speechless as they watch the scene unfold.

Ellen flushes. She steals a quick look at her parents, and
when they don't react, she nods excitedly, and says, "Yes, Tony, I
will marry you."

"Are you out of your mind? You ask her now!" Michael
punches Tony in the arm.

"I'm on a dangerous mission. I might not come back in
one piece."

"Let's get out of here before Ma and Da recover."

131

CHAPTER SEVENTEEN

The rain is coming down in sheets as Tony, Michael and Dania run for the Dennisons' car. They are soaked before they get to the black Oldsmobile. Michael has to back down the road to get onto Adams Street. A huge limb from the neighbor's maple tree falls and blocks the way forward. It misses the car by inches. The trees are being stripped of their leaves; limbs are falling; roof tiles, yard ornaments, and anything not tied down swirl around dangerously—littering the road. It's almost impossible to avoid being hit by projectiles thrown by the force of the wind.

They leave the car at the fairground's gate. The puddle they came through before is now a small river. Fighting the wind, they make their way to Dania's trailer. It takes all Michael's strength to hold the door as each gust threatens to pull it from his hands. Dania goes in first.

"Tell your father he must come," Michael shouts to be heard. "Don't take no for an answer. We're right behind you."

"Yeah, we'll cosh him on the head if we have to," says Tony as he starts to follow her in. "Let's get this over and get out of here."

Suddenly Dania screams, "Hugo, Stop! What are you doing?" Hugo is holding a pillow over Koslov's face. Startled, he looks up, throws the pillow aside, and rushes for the door. Hugo shoves past Dania—knocking her down—and slams into Tony.

They both fly out the door taking Michael with them. All three fall into the mud and are pelted by wind and rain. Tony is stunned.

Hugo jumps up, and before Michael can get to his feet, he punches him in the jaw. Michael goes down. Hugo runs. Sitting in the mud and rain, Michael calls out. "Tony, check on Dania," Tony, covered with mud and still winded from the fall, struggles up the stairs and into the trailer.

Dania is holding her father's hand and crying. Koslov is breathing, but is clearly in distress.

"Don't worry, I'm here now," she croons. "Papa, it's over. Hugo is gone. We came to get you and take you to Michael's house."

Dania and Tony help Koslov down the steps. Tony helps Michael to his feet. Michael rubs his hurt jaw.

"Hugo can sure throw a punch. Let's get home."

At that moment a gust of wind blows them off their feet. They recover quickly. The trailer sways and tips violently.

"Look!"

There is an ear-piercing screech of metal as the bolts and tie downs give and the frame is torn away. They watch as it tips onto its side and is pushed away by the sheer force of the wind. They hear a *SNAP* as the live electrical wire breaks and whips about.

"Let's get out of here." Michael helps Tony hustle Koslov to the car.

The drive back is slow as an array of debris covers the road. On Adams Street, their way is blocked by a downed tree limb.

"Tony, I can't get around it. We'll have to get out and move it out of the way." They jump out of the car, and by lifting one end of the branch they are able to move it enough to get past.

Dania cradles her father and whispers reassuringly. She is frightened by the intense storm, but even more by what might have happened if they had not arrived when they did.

Donal and Moira meet them at the door. "Ellen, take Dania to your room and get her out of those wet things," Moira says. "Tony and Michael, you go upstairs and change, and find something for Mr. Koslov. There will be something in your father's closet. Mr. Koslov, please come into the kitchen by the stove and warm up. I'll put on some tea."

"Ju are most gracious. I'm afraid I don't deserve ju'r hospitality. I was rude not to accept ju'r invitation in the first place."

"You are here now and safe," Donal shows him the way.

In the kitchen Donal and Koslov find chairs by the stove while Moira puts on the kettle for tea. Christopher and Frank can only stare at the stranger in their house.

Michael and Tony come in carrying their wet clothes. Moira puts them on a rack beside the black cast iron stove to dry. Michael hands her his Da's clothes, "Will this do?"

"This is just fine." Moira turns to her guest, "Mr. Koslov, change into these before you get sick."

Koslov takes the offering. Michael shows him where to change and comes back. "We need to get the police. One of the carnival workers, Hugo, was trying to suffocate Mr. Koslov when we got there. They need to find him before he gets away."

"It will have to wait until the storm is over. We've lost electricity, and the phone isn't working."

"And I'm not sending anyone else out in this storm," says Moira.

"I'll go!"

"No. Me, Frank! I'm older."

"I said no one is going, and that's that!" Moira reaches into a cabinet. "We have kerosene lanterns, plenty of ham shoulder and bread for sandwiches. We even have apple pie I can warm up. There might be a slice or two of cheese to go with it."

Koslov returns and hands her his wet things. She puts them on the rack and carries it out of the room.

"Mr. Koslov," says Donal, "Michael was telling us about the man, Hugo. Was he trying to kill you?"

"Yes, that's apparently true. At one time he was like a son. Over the years I have seen him change. He became greedy, wanted to be in control of everyone and everything in the carnival. But his decisions are not always good ones."

"We'll notify the police when we can, but with the phone lines down... If the storm is moving as fast as they say, the worst should be over soon. There will still be rain and the debris, but the wind will stop. You and your daughter must stay here."

"No, no. I will go back to my trailer. I have inconvenienced ju too much already."

Dania enters the kitchen. "Oh, Papa, the trailers are no more. Yours was destroyed by the fire, and the hurricane ripped mine apart." She kneels before him. "We have no place to go right now except here. These are good people. We can trust them to help us."

"Dania, there is much ju do not know about ju'r old papa," He caresses her. "Maybe it is time I spoke of it to ju, and then to the police."

"Papa, you don't have to tell me anything."

"Please, I must do this while I have the courage."

Moira puts cups of tea on the table in front of everyone while Dania takes a seat.

136

"Many years ago I was with the Russian circus. I was a knife thrower. My sister, Katia was part of my act, and her husband, Vicily was on the high wire. One night before the performance I had too much vodka. I was drinking with Vicily. It was stupid, I know, but we were celebrating. Katia had just told him he was to be a father. Vicily went on to do his act. He fell to his death that night, and my sister never forgave me. She left the act." He takes a sip of tea. "In time, Marta replaced her in my act, and she later became my wife." He takes another sip.

"We heard that Katia had a son. When we went to find them, I was told she had died. The boy was in an orphanage in the Ukraine." He takes another sip. "My wife and I adopted the boy and named him Hugo. The war came and went, and then ju were born. My lovely wife, Marta, also died." Koslov wipes the tears running down his face. "I brought ju and Hugo to America, to start a new life."

"You don't have to do this, Papa." Dania brushes away her own tears.

"Please, let me finish. For many years things were good. I bought the carnival. Ju and Hugo were my family, and we were happy. But lately things have changed. Hugo wanted more and more to be in control. On the night of the robbery, I did see who hit me, and I told Hugo. He took it upon himself to find Johnny Russo, to get our money back, and to teach him a lesson. It was Tevia who killed Johnny Russo. Hugo and Tevia said it was an accident. Tevia was only supposed to scare Russo into giving the money back, but he went too far."

He takes a deep breath and continues, "Hugo and Tevia tried to cover it up and blame ju, Michael. When that didn't work, I think Hugo was afraid I might tell Dania and then the police would know. I believe it was Hugo who caused the fire in my trailer."

A long silence fills the kitchen. Even Frank and Christopher are at a loss for words.

Dania hugs her father as tears fill her eyes. "Papa, if we had not gone back for you when we did, Hugo would have killed you."

"We must get the police," says Michael.

"But the storm . . .," Moira doesn't want to hear this."

"We have to, Ma. They have to be stopped before they get away. It may already be too late. Tony and I will go."

"Just wait for the wind to stop."

"We must go before dark. With electricity out all over town and debris everywhere . . ."

"Alright; alright."

"We'll be careful." Michael kisses her on the cheek.

Michael grabs dry coats. Moira hands Tony towels to put down on the seats of the Dennisons' car. "We'll clean the car when this is over." Moira turns to her son. "Christopher, go over and tell the Dennisons we'll be using their car one more time. Tell them it's an emergency. I'll explain later."

Dania helps Michael into his coat. "Please be careful. I don't want anything to happen to you," She wraps her arms around him and kisses him. She releases him with a contented sigh. He takes her by the shoulders and kisses her back, passionately, and with more intensity. He marvels at the sensations he feels by her nearness and the warmth of her kiss. He knows for certain, he's in love with this Russian fortuneteller, and he knows she loves him, too. They are lost for the moment, gazing into each other's eyes.

"Okay you two. That's enough of that!" Tony grabs Michael and shoves him to the door. "We'd better get going or Hugo and Tevia will be long gone."

"You're not leaving me out." Ellen grabs Tony's arm, swings him around, and plants a heated kiss on his full lips.

"Where did you learn to kiss like that?" Tony gasps.

The family is dazed by what they have just witnessed.

"My Dania does not go around kissing boys like that," Koslov states vehemently.

"Neither does my Ellen," Moira says defensively.

"How about we put the kettle back on while we wait? Another cup of tea would be grand with a nice piece of warm apple pie. Eh, Moira?" Donal shakes his head matter-of-factly.

CHAPTER EIGHTEEN

"Get up. We gotta go!" Hugo calls, bursting into the trailer.

"Where? Have you seen the weather?" asks Tevia. "What happened to you? You're drippin' wet and covered in mud."

"Move your ass, Tevia," Hugo shouts. "I had a fight with that Irish *Mick* of Dania's, if you must know. The police will be on their way, and we have to get out of here."

The trailer rocks brutally in the raging gusts of wind.

"What? I don't want to go out there."

"You have a choice: stay here, hope the trailer holds together, and wait for the police to put you in prison for murder; or try to get as far away as possible!"

Tevia stuffs a few things in a small valise and throws on his coat and battered hat. "I don't understand." Then it dawns on him. "Oh no, Hugo, what have you done!"

"Move," yells Hugo. Another gust lifts the trailer off its foundation, and it lists dangerously to one side.

Hugo and Tevia leap from the door to see the remains of Dania's trailer sliding along the ground. They run for Tevia's truck. The rain is coming down in sheets—drenching them as they splash through the mud. "Go out the back way to Craft Street."

Tevia starts the truck. Turning, they see Tevia's trailer roll over and crash into the wrought iron fence surrounding the grounds. Broken pieces caught by the wind swirl through the air as projectiles.

"Hugo, are you going to tell me what's going on?" shouts Tevia.

"I was trying to silence that fool Boris once and for all before he could tell anyone what happened to the Russo kid. Dania came in and caught me. You killed the kid, and I helped cover it up. We'll both go to jail. Storm or no storm, we gotta go!"

They make their way along the streets—dodging falling branches and other debris. A fallen maple blocks their path. Tevia swerves and careens down a side street only to stall out on Hawthorn where the street is flooded.

After listening to Michael and Tony explain about Hugo's attempt on Boris Koslov's life and Tevia's involvement in the death of Johnny Russo, Lieutenant Gillespie puts out an APB for the two. He assigns a couple of men to block off all the main routes out of town and question anyone on the streets. A patrol reports in that an unoccupied truck has been found on Hawthorn Street. Checking the description, they determine it belongs to Tevia.

The lieutenant signals Drew and two others. "We'll search for Hugo and Tevia." He turns to Michael. "Does Hugo know where you live?"

"No, he's never been there," says Michael.

"Good. Go home and stay with your family."

Gillespie and the officers rush past them, down the stairs, and out the door. Tony and Michael leave the station and find their car. Michael slides behind the wheel but doesn't start the engine.

""What are you waiting for?" Tony asks.

"Most of the force is out assisting with other storm-related problems leaving Gillespie with only a few men. It seems to me he's going to need more help. Let's find out." Michael starts the car and follows the patrol car's tail lights.

Hugo and Tevia are searching for another car. The wind is letting up, and they hear the police sirens in the distance.

Hugo checks a garage, but it's empty. "We'd better find something fast."

"I'm cold and wet." Tevia pulls his hat down, and water spills off the brim. "Can't we get out of this rain for a while? Maybe they'll give up lookin' for us."

"Divia mush, they won't give up! Just shut up; you're making me nuts!" The sirens are getting closer. Hugo sees a police car stop at the end of Hawthorn Street and block the road. Officers get out. They watch as another police car blocks the far end of the street near their abandoned truck. A minute later Gillespie pulls up.

Hugo grabs Tevia's coat sleeve and drags him behind some cover. Tevia points toward Gillespie.

"Look, with the police." Tevia points at Michael and Tony.

Gillespie doesn't have time to reprimand Michael and Tony. He only shakes his head and warns them, "Just keep out of our way." He looks up. The sun will soon set and full dark—with no lights anywhere in the city—will descend on the town. Gillespie signals his men to begin. They search the yards, porches, sheds, and garages lining the street in the hope of spotting Hugo and Tevia.

143

Hugo watches from their hiding place. "We have to move now, or we'll get caught." He jabs Tevia. "Keep low. Duck into those trees and brush. Cuyamoi, get a move on!"

Although they try for stealth, their movements are seen. "There they are." The shouts split the late afternoon silence. As the police give chase, Tevia and Hugo run faster. Tony and Michael join the chase close behind Gillespie.

"They're headed for the marsh and the bog," shouts Officer Drew. Michael and Tony split from the rest and head for the other side of the bog.

The marsh is flooded, and Hugo pulls Tevia through knee-deep water, hoping to reach the other side and find a way to escape. Gillespie and Drew see the direction Hugo is going and skirt the marsh to head them off.

Hugo doesn't know the land, so the two run straight on. Thick layers of mud suck at their feet—slowing them down. Each step pulls them deeper into the mire. Twenty feet ahead is the bog.

Michael knows what will happen if the two men continue that way. "Hugo, stop! You're headed for the peat bog."

Hugo stops. Tevia is out of breath. "Cuyamoi," Hugo yells, "Overchay."

"He thinks you're lying, Michael," says Tony.

Gillespie shouts from the other side of the marsh. "Hugo, give it up. Let's talk."

No one wants to follow the men into the marsh. Hugo is very close to the edge of the bog.

Tevia, unable to run in the mud, throws his hands into the air. "I give up. I ain't goin' to die out here." He starts to walk, but he's reached the edge of the bog. He feels himself sink and tries to go back, but every move he makes causes him to sink deeper. He manages to lift one leg only to have the shoe pulled off. He's frantic and grapples for anything to drag himself out. The harder he tries, though, the more he's sucked into the mire.

"Hugo!" The smell is sickening, and with every move he is drawn deeper into it. He raises his chin in an effort to keep the foul stuff out of his mouth, but he panics as he feels it continue to envelope him. He screams, "Help!" A firm hand grabs his collar and slowly hauls him out of the wretched quagmire.

Tevia is hysterical and clings to Hugo like a child. He babbles irrationally; his voice cracks as he sobs uncontrollably.

Hugo pushes him toward Gillespie.

Tevia at first refuses to budge, but in time gathers the courage to make his way to the waiting police. Officer Drew pulls out his handcuffs and walks toward him. Shaking from stress and the cold marsh water, Tevia can barely speak. "Mush has a cormunga in his cover," Tevia blurts to Gillespie. Gillespie nods for Drew to take him away.

"Get him to the station and into some dry clothes," he instructs the officer, "and maybe some hot soup, too."

The two boys are circling back to Gillespie when Michael nudges Tony, "What'd he say?"

"Tevia says Hugo has a gun," explains Tony.

Hugo watches as his friend is led away. He realizes no one is on the west side of the marsh, so he thinks if he can reach the road he might still be able to get away. He moves along—skirting the bog and moving away from the police.

"Hugo, NO!" Tony and Michael see him at the same time.

Gillespie shouts to his men, "Circle around and intercept him." To Hugo, he yells "Don't be a chuccuo. You can't get away!"

145

Hugo stops, but he isn't beaten yet. He reaches into his coat and takes out his revolver. "If I'm going down, I'm going down fighting!"

"Throw the gun away, Hugo! Don't be divia," the lieutenant yells.

Daylight is quickly diminishing. Hugo's response splits the air as he fires a shot that goes wild over their heads. The police have no choice but to return fire. Hugo cannot move fast, but he works his way toward the western bank and to the potential safety of the road.

"Oh God. No!" Michael exclaims. Hugo's path will take him to the edge of the bog where several officers are trying to close in on him. As they approach, one takes aim and shoots. The shot hits Hugo high on his back, and the force of the blow spins him around. He loses his balance and falls. The pain is sharp and burns like a branding iron, but he's determined to get to his feet when another shot hits him in the shoulder and he's shoved forward. He can't regain his footing. The ground is no longer under him, and he feels himself sinking.

He struggles as the water rises around him. He knows he can't make it. He's going to drown in this filthy mire that's all around now. Moving his arms takes more effort than he has, and each movement sinks him deeper into the deadly bog. He gasps for breath, but even that seems to pull him down.

Michael, Tony and the police can only watch and listen as he bellows in Russian. They watch in stunned silence as Hugo raises the gun to his head and pulls the trigger—ending his life before the bog can claim him. The sound reverberates across the water and echoes endlessly into the night as the lifeless body is slowly engulfed by the bog.

CHAPTER NINETEEN

Night has fallen when Donal watches the Dennisons' car pull up. "They're back, everyone! They're back," he calls. Moira hurries from the kitchen, wiping her wet hands on a cloth. She reaches the front door first, almost tripping over Frank and Christopher.

"Where in the name of all that's holy have you been?" she asks, relieved. "You're both a mess and wet through. Get in here, and get those wet things off while I put the kettle on."

Michael walks in the door and takes his jacket and hat off. Tony follows.

"Get upstairs and change. You can tell us all about it when you come down."

Moira watches them climb the stairs. "At least you're home in one piece."

Ellen and Dania come in from the kitchen. Their arms are linked and supporting each other—two young women with one thing in common: love. Everyone gathers in the front room. Frank and Christopher take their places on the floor. Donal and Koslov are seated, and the girls stand by the window.

Michael changes quickly, and Tony borrows things from the boys, although the fit is not great. They join the others, and all eyes turn to them as they enter the room. Ellen can barely hide a laugh when she sees what Tony is wearing. The pants are too big, and the sweater hangs on his small frame.

"I see you borrowed some of Frank's things," Ellen says.

"Ha, ha," Tony replies. She moves to his side and takes his hand. Dania sits on the floor at Michael's feet, leaning against him.

"So, tell us." Donal moves forward in his chair—obviously eager to hear. "Where have you been? Did the police catch Hugo? Why were you gone so long?"

Michael glances at Tony and takes a deep breath. He needs time to gather his thoughts. "I'm sorry, Mr. Koslov. Hugo's dead."

Boris reacts to the news. "I was afraid of that. He was always so stubborn. How did it happen?"

"The trailers were destroyed by the storm, and Hugo and Tevia escaped," Michael begins. "Lieutenant Gillespie and several policemen went to search for them. We went along. They tried to get away in the truck, but they abandoned it, and ran on foot. The police caught up to them at the marsh on Hawthorn Street. You know—close to the peat bog. We tried to talk them into giving up. Hugo pulled Tevia out when he blundered into it. By then Tevia was cold and exhausted and turned himself in. He'd had enough. Hugo wouldn't. He pulled a gun and began shooting, and the police returned fire. He was hit and fell into the bog." Michael concludes—wanting to spare Boris the final details.

Boris struggles to hold back tears. "He was my sister's son, and I loved him like my own. His mother was always very stubborn, too."

Boris needs time to grieve, and Donal keeps him company in case he wants to talk while the others go into the kitchen.

Moira makes tea and fixes a small meal. The women set the table and put out cold, sliced, smoked shoulder, sliced tomatoes, and potato salad with left-over apple pie. Michael and Tony dive right in as Frank and Christopher bombard them with questions. "This is just like one of those crime novels at Kinchela's," Frank announces. Christopher wants to hear all about how the trailers broke up in the storm and demands all the details.

"Mrs. Flannigan, may Ellen and I take a walk around the block?" Tony asks.

"Well, I guess you won't go far dressed like that," she says with a grin. "But be very careful. Ellen, take a flashlight from the drawer. There will be a lot of debris from the storm."

"Why don't Dania and I go too and be their chaperone?" Michael winks at Dania.

"Go on with you then, and get out of my kitchen, or I'll find a job for you," Moira's tone is strong, but there's a smile on her lips. "But not you two," she points to Frank and Christopher as they try to slip away. "A little dish water won't hurt either of you."

It is eerie walking in the dark after the storm. All the street lights are out, and the houses are lit by kerosene lamps or candles. The searching beam of the flashlight Tony carries and the tip of his cigarette that flairs each time he inhales are the only earthly illuminations. Fallen limbs and debris litter the yards, sidewalks, and streets. Cars, houses, pieces of a fence, broken signs, and bits and pieces of unrecognizable items are scattered everywhere. It's a different world than they knew 24 hours ago.

The sky is a blanket of black with millions of stars twinkling peacefully overhead, and an almost-full moon watches over all. The silence is fantastic. There are no cars hurrying past, no music from neighboring houses, no one talking on porches, and the four find themselves whispering so as not to disturb the piety of this newly-created sanctuary.

149

Michael walks arm in arm with Dania. She doesn't want to talk about Hugo or what happened today.

"What are your plans, Dania?"

"Your mother says we can stay at your house for a while."

"That's great, and afterwards?"

"Papa will rejoin the carnival. They have moved south, and he knows where they'll be. That's his life, and they're his people. I talked to him about me staying here." Dania's voice quivers with emotion.

"You would really stay?" Michael stops and turns Dania to face him. He can see the stars reflected in her eyes. "You would stay here, with me?" His heart is racing.

"I could, if you want me to." She looks up at him silhouetted against the star-filled sky.

"Do I have to ask your father for your hand in marriage, or can you just say yes and save me from a nervous breakdown?"

"You should ask him; he might say no, after all you are not Russian," There is a moment of dead silence. Michael is dumbstruck, until Dania bursts into laughter. "That's a joke."

"I'm not so sure. There *are* other concerns. For instance, you're not Catholic."

"Is that so different from our Russian Orthodox? It may take time, but we can work it out, can't we?"

"Well, if we take things one step at a time... Oh, I don't mean I need more time. I know I love you, and I want to spend the rest of my life showing you how much. If it were only me, I would marry you tomorrow, but my parents.. ."

"I understand. Your mother and father have been so kind, and I can see how much they love you and want only the best for you. We can allow them time to get to know me, if it would make you comfortable. Our parents have their ways, both yours *and* mine."

"Looks like it's all settled then," says Michael as he drops down on one knee. "Dania Koslov, will you marry me?"

"Yes, Michael Flannigan, I will marry you," Dania laughs as Michael lifts her and swings her around yelling, "She said 'Yes'!"

Ellen and Tony race back to see what the shouting is about. Michael and Dania are hugging each other, laughing.

"What's up with you two?" Tony asks, but he already knows. He wasn't a gypsy fortune teller but he has seen it coming.

"Dania and I are going to get married," Michael says, his smile stretching from ear to ear.
Ellen jumps up to hug Michael. "I always wanted a sister," Ellen says, turning to hug Dania.

"We have news too," Tony begins cautiously.

"We're getting married, too," Ellen announces excitedly. "We'll get engaged after I graduate high school. Then as soon as I finish my teacher training we can get married."

Michael looks at them both. "Have you told Ma and Da your plans?"

"Not yet," Ellen answers. "She knows Tony asked me and I said yes, so I think she'll approve of our plan."

The young couples finish their walk around the block and return to the house on Chandler Street.

Michael walks in the front door ahead of the others calling out, "Ma, we have something to tell you."

Author Brenda M. Spalding was brought up in "The Lake" area of Newton, Massachusetts. This novel and her mystery, *Broken Branches,* are a reflection of her love of New England and her Irish roots.

She traveled for many years with her military husband. Brenda and her family spent most of their time in England and returned to settle in Bradenton, Florida.

She is on staff at Art Center Sarasota, treasurer for the Sarasota branch of National League of American Pen Women and founder and current president of ABCBooks4Children&Adults, Inc, a networking organization that aims to help fellow authors and illustrators connect and share information.

With several children's books to her credit, she is a strong promoter of children's literacy. She enjoys going to schools and libraries to read her books and talk to children and adults about the benefits of introducing books early in a child's life. Brenda hopes to foster a love of reading in children that will carry over to their later years.

Brenda is active in the arts and enjoys the opera, ballet and the wonderful theaters of Bradenton and Sarasota.

Broken Branches

Brenda M. Spalding

Do you believe in ghosts and spirits? Megan Calloway, a young artist and gallery owner didn't. When her grandmother dies suddenly, Megan travels from her gallery in New York to Salem, Massachusetts.

Rescued by a stranger from a speeding car, Megan feels a timeless connection to her rescuer she can't explain. Together they try to solve the mysteries that surround her Gran's death. Gran's friend, Clarissa, is also murdered. Did she have answers someone didn't want Megan to find out? Who can she trust?

Working with curious riddles left by Megan's ancestors over one hundred and fifty years before, they follow clues leading to the discovery of a lost family treasure and a future they never dreamed of.

"This is a very nice read because of the excellent writing, the unusual story and a satisfying flow of events. It keeps you wondering who the villain could be. In the end when all is resolved, the protagonists win on several levels. Small-sized book, which makes it ideal to toss into the purse and always carry along for a quick page read wherever away from home. This book offers quality writing to do that."

"Passionate and memorable . . . smooth and sensitive, Brenda's book, with its twists and turns and possible murder suspects, will keep you guessing right up to the surprising end! Well-written and hard to put down, this is a novel that can hold its own."

"This was an enjoyable read! It kept my attention right up to the end—never guessing for sure who the bad guys were. A lovely love story with mystery intertwined. I gave it as a gift and received it back to read myself, with a strong recommendation to read! So two excellent ratings! I look forward to reading Brenda's next book!"

More reviews available on Amazon.com

72149716R00088

Made in the USA
Lexington, KY
29 November 2017